'Do you dance

'Not often, Mr Hend

'Almost never.' Paul held her gaze. 'Shall we?'

'Why not?'

Sarah found she could think of several reasons the instant Paul Henderson's hands touched her body. She had only just met the man, for heaven's sake, but her feelings were so powerful she felt she would betray them if she relaxed even slightly. Paul suddenly cleared his throat.

'Do you believe in love at first sight, Sarah Kendall?'

Alison Roberts was born in New Zealand and, she says, 'I lived in London and Washington DC as a child and began my working career as a primary school teacher. A lifelong interest in medicine was fostered by my doctor and nurse parents, flatting with doctors and physiotherapists on leaving home, and marriage to a house surgeon who is now a consultant cardiologist. I have also worked as a cardiology technician and research assistant. My husband's medical career took us to Glasgow for two years, which was an ideal place and time to start my writing career. I now live in Christchurch, New Zealand, with my husband, daughter, and various pets.'

Recent titles by the same author:

A CHANCE IN A MILLION

MUM'S THE WORD

BY
ALISON ROBERTS

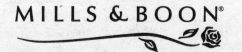

First published in Great Britain 1999
Harlequin Mills & Boon Limited,
Eton House, 18-24 Paradise Road, Richmond, Surrey TW9 1SR

© Alison Roberts 1999

ISBN 0 263 81516 1

Set in Times Roman 11½ on 12 pt.
03-9903-44489-D

Printed and bound in Norway
by AIT Trondheim AS, Trondheim

CHAPTER ONE

SARAH KENDALL was spoiling for a fight.

She knew exactly who her target was and her long legs took the stairs effortlessly two at a time. She was unaware of the heavy disc of her stethoscope, bouncing painfully against her collarbone. The fury which had so far propelled her almost at a run through the busy corridors of Christchurch Central Hospital, across the carefully landscaped buffer zone and into the new, purpose-built, office block of hospital management had not abated even slightly. Although aware that it might be detrimental to her cause, Sarah didn't pause to allow herself time to calm down.

Management had a lot to answer for. The pain caused by the implementation of new health reforms had touched everyone in the medical arena, but this time they weren't going to get away with it. Dr Sarah Kendall was simply not going to let it happen. The angry shove she bestowed on the heavy fire-stop doors was enough to make them swing several times, before closing again.

The wide, carpeted corridor in which she now found herself was obviously enemy territory. Devoid of the normal hospital obstacle course of people, trolleys and equipment, the freedom of movement and the quiet was unnerving. It reeked of power—and control. This was management, all right, Sarah noted scathingly. They were simply on another planet as far as what a hospital was really about.

The secretary who emerged rapidly from her office received what Sarah hoped was a polite nod but her query about an appointment was ignored. Sarah's pace slowed only as she approached the door with a brass plate that read MR P. B. HENDERSON, CHIEF EXECUTIVE OFFICER. Paul Henderson, the new face in senior management. He was rumoured to be sympathetic to the needs of both doctors and patients. Sarah Kendall was in just the mood to test the rumour.

Sarah rapped briskly on the door and opened it, without waiting for a reply. She really didn't care if he was in the middle of a meeting. The way she was feeling right now she was quite prepared to take on any number of management personnel. But Mr P. B. Henderson was alone. Clearly startled by Sarah's abrupt entrance, he remained seated at the massive oak desk which dominated the office, a pen poised in his hand. Sarah pushed the door shut behind her with her foot.

'I will not allow you to take that child away from her mother.' Sarah was pleased that her tone didn't betray the fact that she, too, was startled.

Sarah had expected a grim-faced adversary, grey-haired and pushing retirement, with a pin-striped suit and an attitude to match. Paul Henderson was far too young. Yes, there was a cluster of grey hairs at his temples but the luxurious black waves were far too tousled. He could do with a haircut. His dark

eyes were far too blue, and as for his clothing—
rolled-up shirtsleeves and a loosened collar and tie!

The impression took only seconds but Sarah had
still received no response. Perhaps his attitude was
the only thing left to match her expectations. She
took a step further into the office.

'Alice Forster, Ward 23. Thanks to you, she is
about to be forcibly removed from her mother's
care and I am not going to let that happen.'

'And you are?' The upward movement of Paul
Henderson's eyebrows was the only acknowledgement of Sarah's vehement tone. He appeared un-
ruffled, remaining seated at his desk with his pen
still poised.

'Sarah Kendall. *Dr* Kendall,' Sarah added with
some emphasis. 'Senior registrar, Ward 23. Alice
Forster is my patient, *Mr* Henderson.' Again Sarah
placed emphasis on the title, this time due to the
anger she had no intention of suppressing.

'Would you like to take a seat, *Dr* Kendall?' Paul
Henderson's repetition of Sarah's emphasis was just
enough to let her know that it had annoyed him.
She also noted with startling clarity how the lines
at the corners of his eyes deepened as they narrowed slightly.

'I won't, thanks.' Sarah didn't want to relinquish
her height advantage. Even seated she could see
that Paul Henderson was a large man. His sheer
masculinity was distracting and served to push
Sarah's anger up a notch. She brandished a rather
crumpled sheet of paper, produced from the pocket
of her white coat.

'This is a directive from your office, Mr

Henderson. It states that the hospital intends to up-hold the court's ruling in the case of Alice Forster and—'

The interruption was smooth. 'I believe that di-rective was addressed to the consultant this child was admitted under. Dr Martin Lynch?'

'Alice Forster has been under my care since she was first diagnosed with acute lymphoblastic leu-kaemia nearly twelve months ago. I am much more intimately acquainted with the wider ramifications of this case than is Dr Lynch. In any case, he agrees with me.'

'That's not the impression I get.' The tone was still controlled. Smug, Sarah decided. No, more than that. Arrogant.

'Dr Lynch agrees with me in principle—as any-body with even a remote interest in humanitarian issues would. He is not, however, willing to take a stand and defy a management directive.'

'Which you are.'

'Obviously.' Sarah met his direct stare. Not only arrogant, she decided, but also patronising. Typical management, after all. She felt a flash of relief when he broke their eye contact, but as his gaze flicked down and then up again she saw the beginnings of a smile and remembered what she was wearing.

While a great hit with the children on the ward, her Bart Simpson sweatshirt, jeans and the large, yellow, sun-shaped badge on her white coat which said HI, I'M DOCTOR SARAH were not exactly ap-propriate in the present circumstances. The feeling of being patronised intensified and Sarah leaned forward over the large desk, speaking more quietly.

'I am not only prepared to defy management. I will, if necessary, create adverse publicity for this hospital by defying the court's ruling that this child be removed from her mother's custody.'

'The issue is not the removal of the child from her mother.' Paul Henderson's hint of a smile vanished and his gaze returned to meet Sarah's hostile glare. 'It is about the granting of a father's rights of access to his terminally ill daughter and his contribution to her welfare.'

Sarah's voice rose sharply. 'Alice's welfare can only be served by remaining with her mother in a safe environment and receiving the medical care essential to her well-being.'

'Her medical care is going to be provided by her father. As I understand it, he has hired private medical staff at some considerable expense. He—'

Sarah interrupted angrily, her words tumbling over each other. 'This child has been cared for twenty-four hours a day by her mother from the moment she became ill. Alice was only five when that happened. She had just started school and she charmed everyone she met. She had curly blonde hair, big blue eyes and a smile that never quit. We all fell in love with her and were just as happy as her mother when she went into her first remission.' Sarah straightened, her lips pressed firmly together.

Paul Henderson was silent. He fiddled slowly with the pen he still held but his eyes were fixed on Sarah's face. Sarah stared at his hands as the long fingers toyed with the pen. Surgeon's hands, Sarah noted abstractedly—or maybe a musician's. After the briefest silence she turned and walked slowly towards the large window of the office. She stared, unseeing, at the magnificent view it framed.

'It didn't last, of course. I've lost count of the number of times they've been back. They've both suffered through countless painful and unpleasant experiences. Chemotherapy, infections, blood tests, bone-marrow biopsies. But Alice managed to keep smiling. We all hoped against hope that the bone-marrow transplant would succeed even though it wasn't a perfect match. The graft versus host disease put an end to that hope. The steroids needed to control that have swollen Alice's face until you can hardly recognise her. She has bleeding into her gut and joints.

'We can control the pain but she can't move very much. She had already lost all her hair from the chemotherapy.' Sarah's voice dropped almost to a whisper. 'The smile is still the same. But it doesn't appear very often now and it only appears for one person. And that's her mother.'

Sarah whirled from her position at the window. Her tone became harsh. 'Her father's, Simon Forster's, interests are purely his own. He's in local politics, wants to move into the national arena and this looks like good P.R.' Sarah strode back to the desk. 'For the sake of publicity he intends to haul a dying child away from the only person important to her into the care of total strangers—'

'He's hardly a stranger. He's the child's father. We have no business judging his motives.' Paul's tone was finally angry. He stood up as he spoke. Sarah found her gaze travelling up—and up. At well over six feet Paul Henderson towered over her, but Sarah wasn't about to let herself be intimidated.

'Simon Forster walked out on Isobel Forster when Alice was less than two years old. You're talking about a man who has refused any contact or—'

'Or been refused any contact, perhaps?'

Sarah talked over the interruption. 'Or any financial support for her or her mother, even when Alice became ill.' Sarah snorted incredulously. 'You're talking about a man who even refused to allow himself to be tested as a possible bone-marrow donor when his daughter's illness became critical!'

Paul Henderson walked around the side of his desk. 'I admit it's a tragic story. And one that you have portrayed with admirable eloquence. Unfortunately it has nothing to do with the present situation.'

'How can you say that?' Sarah was so incredulous her voice squeaked.

'This is a hospital, Dr Kendall, in case you've forgotten. We are concerned with a patient's medical condition and care. We do not have the luxury of making decisions or interfering with social issues, marriage guidance or custodial disputes. This is up to other authorities.'

Paul Henderson raised his hand sharply to pre-empt Sarah's interruption. 'As I understand the situation, there is nothing more we can do for the child that cannot be effectively managed outside the hospital. Many would argue that the terminal stage of anybody's illness is preferably managed in a non-medical environment. If the parents choose such a course we have to support it where possible. We cannot afford to keep beds open purely on moral or social grounds—particularly in direct opposition to the ruling of a family court which has presumably considered *both* sides of this story.'

Sarah's brown eyes flashed. 'Of course—it all comes down to money, doesn't it, Mr Henderson?' She took a step closer to Paul. 'Well, let me tell you, there are people lying in those beds—not accounting sheets. Perhaps if you actually took some notice of that you might do a better job at management of a hospital.'

Paul closed the gap between them. 'Perhaps you should try being a doctor instead of a social worker, Sarah Kendall. For your information there's a little more involved in management than counting pennies.'

With only a matter of inches between them, they glared at each other. Sarah's beeper sounded but she ignored the intrusion. She tossed back her hair with an angry shake of her head.

'And, for your information, Mr Henderson, there's a little more to being a doctor than counting pills!'

Sarah turned on her heel and stormed out of the office, her beeper punctuating the silence behind her. Still seething, she made her way rapidly down the stairs. She should have known better than to expect a change of heart from management. Angry as she still was, Sarah was also acutely aware of another emotion, threatening to override her anger. She recognised it just as her beeper sounded for the third time.

Exhilaration. That's what it was. The sparks that had flown in the office of Mr P. B. Henderson were still with her. There was something about that man—quite apart from his blatant physical attributes. Or perhaps it was simply the atmosphere. Perhaps Sarah was just more aggressive than she had ever realised. She rarely became embroiled in heated discussion let alone all-out verbal battles. Sarah couldn't help a wry grin to herself as she entered the main hospital wing and made her way to the nearest telephone. Perhaps she should indulge herself a little more often.

Paul Henderson shook his head in amazement. He remained in his office, staring down from his window, long after the figure of Sarah Kendall had been swallowed by the main hospital wing. That had to have been the most extraordinary encounter he had ever had. Just who the hell was Sarah Kendall—apart from being, without doubt, the most attractive woman he had ever seen?

'Feisty little thing,' he murmured, and chuckled out loud at the thought of how she would respond to the description. How old was she? In those clothes she could pass for a teenager. The tightly fitting jeans had advertised a coltish length and slimness to those legs, but even that ridiculous, shapeless sweatshirt had failed to hide the curves of a mature woman. And that hair! Bathed in the sunlight from the window, it had seemed to be sprayed with golden glitter and so straight it rippled like silk when she shook her head. She could do with a haircut, though, Paul mused. The soft fringe was so long it almost got caught in those magnificent eyelashes. Any longer and it might hide those extraordinary brown eyes...

With some difficulty Paul Henderson cleared his mind of the overwhelming impressions with which Sarah Kendall had left him. His anger was gone and he recognised that it had been born of embarrassment—embarrassment that he'd had no knowledge of the background issues of this case and hadn't made any effort to find out. He prided himself on seeing both sides of an issue, but it hadn't occurred to him that in this case one of the sides had its own sides that both deserved consideration. Never mind that he was snowed under with fending off a strike by the cleaners, that the papers were about to publish damning figures about current waiting lists for surgery and that the extension to the emergency department had mysteriously doubled in cost since the estimates. It was no excuse to lose sight of what a hospital was really about.

Wasn't that exactly what he had told himself he could and would do when he took this position? With his background he was one of the few who would be able to see both sides of every dispute, be able to mediate and create a co-operation between medical and management staff which could become a shining example to the rest of the nation. If this was an indication of his success so far then Dr Sarah Kendall was absolutely right. He was losing sight of what hospital beds were really about. And it wasn't good enough. He pressed the button on his intercom.

'Sally? Get Martin Lynch on the phone for me, please.'

The persistent beeping of Sarah's pager had been a call from the emergency department. Sarah found herself listening to a brief summary of a case referred urgently to hospital by a GP—a six-year-old girl who had become progressively more unwell since yesterday and now looked like a case of meningococcal meningitis. Sarah moved quickly towards Emergency. Six years old. The same age as Alice Forster. Sarah bit her lip. If she was going to do her job properly she would just have to forget about Alice for the moment.

Was Paul henderson right? Was she too emotionally involved with her patients and did that make her function less effectively in her primary role as a physician? It was an issue that needed some thought but now was not the appropriate time. Or place.

The emergency department registrar showed Sarah to the cubicle where a small girl lay curled up miserably on a bed. Her eyes were screwed shut. Sarah smiled at the very anxious-looking parents and laid a hand on the child's forehead.

'Hi, Charlotte. My name is Sarah and I'm a doctor. I'd like to have a look at you and see if we can't make you feel a bit better.'

The feverish feel of the child's skin was expected after the telephone call but the registrar hadn't mentioned the faint rash around Charlotte's eyes. It was an unusual rash, like tiny blood spots under the skin. Sarah touched it gently. A possible sign of meningitis, it could also be caused by a transient rise in venous pressure after an event such as vomiting.

'When did she start vomiting?' Sarah directed the question at the child's mother.

'Last night. Just once. But she's been sick several times this morning. It makes her cry—she says it hurts her head.'

'Did you notice anything about the way she vomited?'

'Well, yes. It was different than last time—but that was ages ago. She's normally very well.'

'How was it different?'

'Kind of, well—it went a long way.'

Sarah nodded. Projectile vomiting was another prominent feature of meningitis. She leaned closer to Charlotte.

'Does the light hurt your eyes, sweetheart?'

Charlotte nodded slightly but then whimpered in pain.

'Your head still hurts a lot too, doesn't it?'

Sarah received no response. The child turned her face away into the pillow. Sarah glanced up at the emergency department registrar, Matt Warnock.

'Kernig's sign?'

'Positive.'

'OK. I'll just check that.'

With plenty of encouragement, and help from a nurse, Sarah turned Charlotte gently but firmly onto her back. Placing her hand under the back of the child's head, Sarah attempted to flex Charlotte's neck. The girl's whole trunk lifted from the bed and she began to cry miserably. Gently Sarah replaced her head on the pillow. She completed her examination as quickly as possible, checking Charlotte's abdomen, listening to her chest and looking at the rest of her skin. She found nothing to change her initial impression and moved to the end of the bed to speak to the parents.

'It seems quite likely that Charlotte is suffering from meningococcal meningitis. We'll admit her immediately and I'll do a lumbar puncture as soon as we get her up to the ward. Along with the blood tests, which have been taken here, that will let us know exactly what bug we're dealing with, but we'll start intravenous antibiotic treatment straight away. We don't need to wait for the results.'

Charlotte's mother spoke in a broken whisper. 'People die from meningitis.'

'It's a serious illness,' agreed Sarah, 'and sometimes it progresses too quickly to be managed, but Charlotte's already been ill for twenty-four hours and her condition is not too serious yet. Antibiotics are extremely effective with this disease. I'm confident we'll get on top of things pretty quickly. Would you both like to come up to the ward with her?'

Charlotte's mother nodded. She turned to her husband. 'Could you dash home and get Charlotte's nightie and some of her toys? Don't forget Boo-Boo!' She looked at Sarah apologetically. 'That's her favourite bear. She never sleeps without him.' Her voice wobbled and tears looked imminent.

Sarah stood back to make room for Charlotte's bed to pass. She touched the child's cheek. 'I'll see

you upstairs in a few minutes, sweetheart.
Mummy's going to come with you, OK?'

Sarah reached for the telephone as they left but
motioned for Charlotte's father to wait.

'Do you have other children?' She pushed the
buttons on the phone as she spoke.

'Yes—two. Her brother's at school and we left
the younger one with a neighbour.'

'Right. We may need— Excuse me.' Sarah
turned her attention to the phone. 'Angela? I've got
a six-year-old, Charlotte Newman, on her way up.
Probable meningococcal meningitis. Could you
set up for a lumbar puncture, please?' She listened
for a few seconds, nodding. 'That's right.
Benzylpenicillin, IV. We'll start as soon as we've
completed the puncture. I'll be there in five
minutes.'

Hanging up the phone, Sarah turned back to Mr
Newman. 'We should get the results of the tests
within a few hours, and if we're correct in the diagnosis it would be advisable for all family members to have a prophylactic course of antibiotics—
just to protect you all from catching a disease
you've been in close contact with. I'll ring your GP
as soon as we have the results and arrange things
if you can get in touch with your clinic later.' She
smiled. 'I'd better let you go and collect Boo-Boo.
I'm sure Charlotte will be keen to see him.'

The paediatric department was like no other in the
hospital. It was a melting pot of specialties, with
the paediatricians working with or alongside consultants from virtually every area. Parents were en-

couraged to stay with their children where possible
and formal visiting hours held little authority. With
the number of nursing staff, visiting teachers, physio and occupational therapists, as well as doctors,
the traffic of adults was constant. But it was the
children, of course, who held centre stage.

Paediatrics was probably the busiest, definitely
the brightest and frequently the noisiest department
in the hospital. The specialty was demanding, difficult, exhausting, heart-breaking and enormously
rewarding. It was an area either loved or hated. The
ones who hated it moved rapidly into other depart-
ments. Sarah Kendall had stayed.

The twin wards 22 and 23 were spacious and
brightly decorated, the atmosphere relaxed and
friendly. Sarah walked past a huge mural of
Maurice Sendak's "Wild Things", having their
rumpus on the walls of Ward 23, as she made her
way towards the treatment room. As she passed the
central desk area Angela Grant, the nurse manager,
looked up from the paperwork she was sorting with
one hand. The other was balancing a wailing six-
month-old baby on her hip.

'They're almost ready for you, Sarah. How did
you go in the lion's den?'

'Things got a bit heated. I'm not sure I did much
good.'

'What's Paul Henderson like?'

Sarah smiled without amusement. 'Tall, dark,
handsome and—bureaucratic. Bottom line is that
we can't afford to keep beds open on social grounds
and custody disputes are none of our business.'

Angela groaned. 'Typical management, then?'

Sarah shrugged. 'I'm not sure I'd call him typical.' She glanced up as a red light came on over a door near the central desk. 'They're ready for me. I'll catch you later.'

'No, I'll catch you.' Angela grinned. 'Guess who's pulled out his IV line again?'

It was Sarah's turn to groan. 'Not Anthony again?' She stooped to cover her shoes with surgical bootees and to don a gown, before entering the treatment room. She was quite happy to postpone for as long as possible the prospect of dealing with the hyperactive three-year-old boy they were treating for pneumonia.

Charlotte Newman lay in the same position in which Sarah had last seen her. Two nurses were busy, one talking to Charlotte, the other making preparations for the procedure. Like the nurses, Charlotte's mother wore a gown and mask but Sarah could see the fear in her eyes.

'Why don't you sit over here, Mrs Newman? That way you can hold Charlotte's hand.' Sarah smiled at the girl, reaching for a mask and bent to her eye level, before tying it on.

'This won't take long, darling. I'm going to give you an injection in your back. It won't hurt much because I've got special medicine to make it go numb. It's very important because it's going to help us find out what bugs are making you sick and then we're going to give you some more medicine to bop them all off. OK?'

Rewarded with the smallest hint of a smile, Sarah stroked the girl's cheek. 'I think you're a real champion, Charlotte. I'll bet your mum's really proud of you.'

Sarah nodded to Judith, the senior nurse, waiting to assist her and then turned to the basin to scrub up. She cast her eye over the adjacent trolley as she did so.

'What gauge needle have you got there, Judith?'

'Twenty.'

'Right. Have you checked that the stylet fits the needle barrel?'

'Not yet.'

'OK, I'll do that.' Sarah took the towel that Judith held with a pair of forceps. She dried her hands and then put on the surgical gloves.

'You prep her while I go over this.' Sarah began to check the instruments and drugs on the trolley.

Once she was ready both nurses held Charlotte in position, lying on her left side. Her back was bright orange from the disinfectant and a sterile drape exposed only her lower spine.

Sarah counted and then carefully introduced the needle into the space between the third and fourth lumbar vertebrae. Having infiltrated the area with local anaesthetic, she changed to the needle and stylet. She angled the needle slightly as she advanced slowly, withdrawing the stylet frequently to check for the emergence of cerebrospinal fluid.

The staff kept up a running commentary of encouragement for both Charlotte and her mother, but Sarah fell silent as she felt the decrease in resistance to the needle that indicated she was in the correct position. When she withdrew the stylet completely, however, the clear fluid dripped only reluctantly.

Sarah held her breath as she rotated the barrel of the needle, without altering its position. The drips came more readily and Sarah breathed a sigh of relief as she collected the sample into the required three serial tubes. She replaced the stylet and then withdrew the whole system from the child's back. She pressed a sterile swab to the puncture site and leaned over her patient.

'You know something, Charlotte? I was right. You are a real champion.'

The insertion of the IV line was completed with minimal trauma and Sarah was delighted when the first dose of antibiotics had been administered. For the moment the invasive procedures were over. She looked at Judith.

'Have you got a single room available?'

Judith nodded and Sarah smiled at Mrs Newman. 'There's a bed in the room for you as well. We'll get Charlotte comfortable and we can keep the room dark for the moment. Judith here will be keeping a close eye on her and I'll be in and out quite often.' She turned to the nurse.

'We'll need half-hourly neurological observations. Response to command, hand grip on both sides, movement of feet, pupillary reflexes—the usual line-up. Blood pressure and heart rate, of course, and I want plasma and urine electrolytes monitored carefully. Fluids need to be restricted at present as well.'

Sarah left them to transfer her young patient to her room and stopped back at the central desk to write up her admission notes. She would have to come back later to fill in details missing from the admission history. Right now both mother and child needed a rest.

Angela appeared, still carrying the baby who now bestowed a beaming smile on Sarah. Sarah smiled back but felt a familiar wrench. Six-month-old baby Jack was waiting for surgery to start the reconstructive process on a seriously cleft lip and palate. His smile was split in the middle right up to his nose. The plate he had worn over his gums and palate for months in preparation for the surgery had wires which extended out over both cheeks.

The surgery was booked for early the following week. Jack was in for the day for assessment to check that he was fit for an anaesthetic and to have blood tests. He was also to be seen by an ENT surgeon due to the repeated ear infections to which he was prone because of the deformity.

Sarah smiled again. 'You're going to look like a completely different baby next week, Jack. Isn't that great?'

Angela sat the baby on the desk beside Sarah. 'How did your puncture go?'

'Brilliantly. She's a great kid.' Sarah moved the test tubes beside her out of the baby's reach. 'Can you get these off to the lab straight away?'

'Of course. Have you seen Anthony yet?'

'No.' Sarah twirled her chair and scooted across to the trolley that housed patient notes. 'I want to check this morning's lab results. I think he can go onto oral therapy now.'

'They haven't been filed yet.' Angela riffled through an in-basket of result forms. 'His temperature was normal this morning.'

'Good. He'll be much happier when he's mobile.'

'Ah, but will we?'

Sarah grinned. 'You'll cope.' Standing, Sarah stretched her back. 'Why is it so quiet in here at the moment? Not that I'm complaining!'

'It's 2 p.m.,' Angela pointed out. 'Rest time.'

From 1 till 2:30 p.m. the ward assumed a mantle of peace that staff tried hard to enforce. It was the only time of day that visitors were not welcome and staff visits were kept to emergencies only.

'I suppose Alice is asleep?' Sarah queried.

Angela nodded. 'So's Isobel. I just checked on them.'

'I'll leave visiting till later, then.' Sarah sighed. 'I wish I had some good news to give them.' She glanced away. 'What's Michael doing out of bed?'

Angela echoed Sarah's sigh. 'He's really down today.'

Sarah eyed the boy, sitting slouched in a wheelchair at the far end of the corridor. Ten years old, Michael was having a difficult time, coming to terms with the amputation of his leg following a car accident. Convinced he would never play his beloved football again, he had withdrawn into angry, uncooperative behaviour. A stump infection had delayed his discharge and Michael refused to be encouraged by anyone.

'Right. It's time we did something about this.' Grinning at Angela, Sarah reached up to a high shelf and produced a black plastic skull cap complete with large round ears. She jammed it on her head and walked purposely towards Michael.

Dropping to her haunches beside the boy in the wheelchair, Sarah eyed the quiet expanse of floor in front of them.

'I'll bet you can't go faster than me down to the end of the corridor even if I just walk.'

'Course I can.' Michael's tone was disinterested but Sarah noted that both hands inched towards the top of his wheels.

'Bet you can't!'

'Can too. Even if you run.'

'I'm not going to run.'

Michael eyed her suspiciously. 'Promise?'

'Of course.' Sarah tucked her hair behind her ears. 'Running inside is not ladylike. Are you on, then?'

'I guess.'

'Right. Ready? Go!' Sarah started slowly but rapidly increased her pace to try and keep up. She broke into a run as they passed the central desk but Michael was way ahead of her. He braked hard as he reached the last door and turned swiftly. Sarah slowed to a walk again but not quickly enough.

'Cheat!' The delighted crow echoed down the corridor. 'You ran! I saw you!'

'Yeah. I guess I'm not so ladylike.' Catching Angela's eye, she saw the smile as well as a disapproving head shake. The grin on Michael's face was so good to see that Sarah ignored the silent remonstration of her breach of rest time. She grinned at Michael. 'Want to go again?'

'Sure.'

They turned to assume starting positions but Sarah's smile faded as she saw the group of people advancing on them. All men, all well dressed. All heading for Alice Forster's room. It spelled trouble.

'I'm sorry, Michael. I'll have to do this later.'

Michael shrugged, his smile gone. Sarah leaned close to his ear.

'Next time I'm going to run as fast as I can and I'll beat the wheels off you.' She caught the flicker of a grin as she moved after the men. She saw that Isobel Forster had emerged from her daughter's room and had closed the door protectively behind her. As Sarah passed the lifts the doors opened. Paul Henderson and Martin Lynch appeared beside her. Sarah was moving at a rapid pace but Paul Henderson's long strides overtook her in no time.

'Let me handle this, Dr Kendall.'

'No way,' Sarah snarled. 'I know what they're here for.'

Paul caught Sarah's arm and forced her to a halt. 'I'm quite aware of why they're here and I'm asking you to let me handle what is essentially a management concern.'

Sarah jerked her arm free but she could still feel the pressure of his fingers. She noticed the transformation effected by the neatly knotted tie, recently combed hair and the tweed jacket now worn by the manager. He would fit right in with all the other sharks now gathering.

'You want me to stand back so you can help them destroy the only quality left in a child's life.' Sarah deliberately kept her voice down but Paul's words were even quieter.

'No. I'm asking you to stand back because they may be less than impressed, being ordered about by someone wearing a Bart Simpson sweatshirt and Mickey Mouse ears!'

Sarah gasped. She had completely forgotten her headgear. She snatched it off but found she could only follow in the wake of the two new arrivals. She joined the edge of the group now gathered in front of Alice's room as introductions were finishing between Simon Forster, his solicitors and the hospital representatives.

'I'm sorry, gentlemen,' Paul Henderson informed the group. 'We've had to change our plans. Alice Forster's condition has deteriorated to the point where we are unable to discharge her.'

Sarah's eyes widened with alarm. Why had she not been informed? Catching Isobel's eye, she realised that Alice's mother was just as surprised as she was. What was going on?

'That was not the case when we spoke this morning, Mr Henderson.' The solicitor's tone was wary.

'Medical conditions such as this are subject to rapid change. A review was called for early this afternoon and it is the opinion of the paediatric consultants involved that the child should not be moved. Is that correct, Dr Lynch?'

Martin Lynch nodded. The older man caught Sarah's astonished gaze and his look warned her to remain silent.

Paul spoke more firmly. 'Management is going to back this decision and is quite prepared to take the case back to court if necessary.'

Sarah caught Isobel's eye again and they exchanged another look of astonishment.

'That is exactly what will be necessary,' the solicitor said crisply. His associates nodded their agreement. 'I can assure you the resultant publicity will not be welcomed by the hospital, Mr Henderson. It will also be expensive.'

Paul Henderson stepped closer to the speaker. He looked down at the younger man. 'I doubt very much that the publicity will be welcomed by your client either.'

'Simon Forster is a father who is simply desperate for a last chance to be with his child. He has been unable to overcome the obstructions placed in his way. The court has already demonstrated its sympathy to his cause.'

Paul lowered his voice. 'They may be less sympathetic when they learn that Simon Forster has made no effort up till now to be with his child and, in fact, refused to allow himself to be tested as a possible bone-marrow donor, which was his daughter's only hope of a cure to this disease.'

The look that Simon Forster received from his legal advisors suggested that no mention had been made of these facts. Paul stepped back to stand beside Isobel Forster.

Sarah was stunned. She was quite sure that Alice Forster's condition had not changed. She watched as Simon Forster and his legal representatives retreated. Martin Lynch excused himself and Isobel returned to her daughter's room. Left alone with Paul Henderson, Sarah felt awkward.

'What made you change your mind?'

'Perhaps management isn't quite as unfeelingly bureaucratic as you'd like to believe, Dr Kendall.'

'Perhaps it's more a case of the squeaky door getting some oil,' Sarah responded.

'Are you suggesting that I should not have responded to your intervention?' The hint of the smile Sarah had glimpsed that morning was now much more developed. 'Would you like to argue your way into changing the situation again?'

Sarah grinned reluctantly. 'No, thanks. What I meant was perhaps you just need enlightenment on other cases as well.'

'Are you offering?'

Sarah looked up to meet an intense gaze. They were standing close together. Almost as close as they had been that morning. The sparks were no longer flying but there was a heat Sarah felt very tempted to stir up.

'What do you mean?'

'Have dinner with me. Let loose a few more of your views on management. I'll see if I can defend my side of the war zone.'

Sarah tossed back her hair. 'That's a challenge I'll have to accept. I can only see that as my duty as a doctor.'

Paul Henderson smiled again. 'I'll ring you later. Right now I think you have a patient waiting. It looks serious.'

Sarah looked around to see Michael, glowering at her from his wheelchair. She hid a smile.

'You're right. It is serious. You'll have to excuse me.' Sarah raised her Mickey Mouse ears in farewell, before settling them firmly back onto her head.

'OK, Michael. There is absolutely no way you're going to beat me this time.'

CHAPTER TWO

IT WAS an afternoon for triumphs. Large and small.

Flushed with the success of beating Sarah three times in a row, Michael had even greeted his physiotherapist, Cheryl, with a smile when the increase in activity signalled the end of the ward's rest period.

Cheryl caught Sarah's eye in surprised acknowledgement of the boy's mood change. Sarah grinned in response and then crouched beside Michael.

'We haven't finished this contest yet,' she warned. Her gaze flicked up to meet Cheryl's again. 'What is it today, Cheryl? Crutches?'

'Sure is.' Cheryl's cheerful tone belied the struggle she was having, working with Michael. Up till now he had refused point blank to even attempt walking, and Sarah knew that the last effort on the part of the long-suffering physio had resulted in the crutches being hurled across the room. His artificial leg was already being made but Michael's attitude made its immediate usefulness questionable.

'Right.' Sarah nodded. 'That's great. Can you bring up a pair my size tomorrow as well?'

Cheryl nodded, bemused. Sarah gave Michael a stern look.

'That's going to be tomorrow's race, kid. You and me. On crutches. Same time, same place.'

Sarah rose smoothly and waved, without giving Michael any time for a response. 'See you then.'

The visit to Alice Forster's room was a time of quiet celebration between mother and doctor, a release from the stress of the last few days, which had escalated ever since they had learned of Simon Forster's legal bid to gain custody of his daughter. Alice was still asleep. Sarah bent and kissed the puffy cheek of the tiny girl and automatically checked her subcutaneous infusion line, running her finger gently down the tubing. It was a pump system that allowed Alice to control the amount of pain relief she received. So far, it was working well.

Isobel watched quietly from her position at the window and Sarah moved to give her a hug. Over the many traumatic admissions the two women had become good friends and Sarah shared the heartbreak of this current and probably final time they had together.

She looked at the young mother with concern. 'You look all in, Isobel. You should take a break while Alice is asleep. One of the nurses could stay with her.'

'I need to be here when she wakes up,' Isobel replied quietly. 'I don't want her to ever open her eyes and not see that I'm here with her.'

Sarah hugged her again. 'And that's exactly where you're going to be. You're safe now.'

'Thanks to you. What did you say to that manager to make them change their minds?'

Sarah grinned a little shamefacedly. 'Quite a few things.' her grin faded. 'I didn't think he had listened but I was wrong—thank goodness.'

Isobel sighed. 'It would have been nice to take her home one last time. But after this I couldn't cope—not without your support and knowing we're in a place we're safe.'

Sarah glanced around the small room. 'It looks like a home to me.'

The walls had been covered with posters and pictures drawn by Alice's classmates. Cards from friends and colourful mobiles hung from strings across the room. A television set and VCR stood in a corner, a stack of her favourite movies and recordings of shows beside it. The entertainment was often a vital distraction in the long hours of a sleepless night.

A borrowed trolley was covered in books and games, stuffed toys and dolls sat in heaps on the floor and the end of Alice's bed and a procession of plastic ducks covered the entire window-sill. Ducks were a huge favourite with Alice. A treasured soft yellow velvet one was tucked in its usual spot in the crook of her right elbow. *The Story of Ping* was lying face down on her bed, still open at the point at which she had fallen asleep. Sarah smiled. She had read that one to Alice herself on several occasions.

'Oh, I forgot to give you something this morning.' Sarah fished in her white coat pocket and carefully unfolded a piece of glossy paper. 'It's a fantastic picture of a duckling. I found it in a medical journal, of all places. I was reading it at breakfast.'

'She'll love it.' Isobel smiled her thanks.

'Have you seen any ducks today?' The window of Alice's room overlooked the river. A large armchair was positioned so that many hours could be comfortably spent with Alice in her mother's arms, watching the activity near and on the water.

'No. I've been too worried to— What on earth is that awful noise?'

Sarah's eyes widened in horror. 'Somebody's certainly having a good wobbly.'

The crescendo of shrieks was appalling.

'Good grief!' Isobel cast an anxious glance at Alice who stirred slightly.

Sarah thought of Charlotte Newman, trying to rest in her darkened room. This was not going to help.

Excusing herself, Sarah marched purposefully towards the dreadful noise. She knew it was Anthony even before she entered the playroom and found the large three-year-old hurling toys and screaming. His mother was in tears, pleading with Anthony to 'be a good boy and swallow your medicine'. A grim-faced Judith stood beside her, holding a medicine glass.

Sarah couldn't help grinning at Judith. 'Not much wrong with his lungs now, is there?'

Judith spoke through clenched teeth. 'I believe it was your idea he went onto oral therapy?'

'Yeah.' Sarah rolled her eyes and took the glass of pink liquid from Judith. 'Get Mum out of here for a minute, Jude. I'll see what I can do.'

Left alone, Sarah ignored the boy and his tantrum. Instead, she ran to a stuffed bear which Anthony had been beating against the table, before discarding it with force.

'Oh, no!' she said in tones of horror. 'Poor

teddy!' Sarah threw herself onto her knees, cradling the bear, aware that Anthony was watching her. His volume had increased, if anything, on finding he was being ignored.

'Have you got a broken arm? Leg? Is it your ear?' Sarah focused her attention on the bear. 'I have just what you need, teddy.'

The packet of jellybeans that came out of her pocket signalled an abrupt end to Anthony's screams. He moved closer.

'First you have to take your medicine,' Sarah told the bear firmly. She held the small plastic container against the toy's mouth and pretended to tip. 'Well done! What colour jellybean would you like? Red? Green? Ah, a blue one.'

'Red.'

Sarah turned her head quizzically. 'Oh, would you like a red jellybean, Anthony?' She feigned surprise. 'You have to swallow the medicine first, like teddy did. Can you do that?'

After hesitating briefly, Anthony nodded. As Sarah dispensed the red jellybean she held up the empty container and grinned triumphantly at the window of the playroom where both Anthony's mother and Judith were watching. The boy's mother rushed back to her son with relief.

Judith caught Sarah's eye. 'Expect a beep in about six hours when he needs his next dose.'

'Hmm. He looks almost well enough for discharge, don't you think?'

'Absolutely.' Judith chuckled. 'Martin Lynch is down in the office. Have a chat to him about it. He was looking for you.'

Sarah bit her lip. 'He probably wants to discuss the little scene I had with management this morning.'

'Could be.' Judith gave her an unsympathetic shove. 'Go and get it over with—and don't forget about Anthony.'

'As if I could.'

Sarah found her consultant in the staff kitchen. She followed his example and made herself a cup of coffee. Realising she had missed lunch, she also raided the biscuit tin. 'You seem to have made quite an impression on Paul Henderson.' The older man's tone was amused.

'Oh?' Sarah concentrated on stirring her coffee. She noted the thump and increase in her heart rate at the mention of his name. A vivid image of him, towering over her in his office, sprang to mind and Sarah felt the heat of a blush prickle the back of her neck. 'I'm surprised he changed his mind about Alice.'

'I'm not.' Martin Lynch smiled at his senior registrar. 'But I'll say no more about that.' He shook his head gently. 'I'm going to miss having you around, Sarah. Have you decided what you're going to do next month when your run with us finishes?'

'No.' Sarah swallowed the last piece of her biscuit. 'There's an opening in Neonatal Intensive Care but I'm not sure I want to go back there. It's pretty draining stuff. I'm filling in there with some nights on call at the moment and even that's a bit much.'

Martin Lynch nodded. 'Working with children

and babies is emotionally difficult. And you do tend to get too involved, Sarah. It's not good for you.'

'And not good for my patients?'

'I didn't say that. You're a superb doctor, Sarah. The best registrar I've ever had. But what sort of life have you got for yourself? The way you get so involved here it makes me wonder whether you have any personal life at all.'

'It's terrific,' Sarah assured him. 'Every chance I get I'm working on my research papers for you and those fascinating case reports you keep wanting me to write up and submit to the journals.'

Martin laughed. 'Don't forget the presentation you're doing for Friday's lunchtime meeting.' He sobered quickly. 'Is it that bad, Sarah?'

Sarah sighed. 'I'm beginning to wonder.'

'Maybe you should take a few weeks off at the end of this run—have a think about what direction you want to go in. I'll do whatever I can to help you when you do decide. My offer of part-time work at my private clinic is still open, you know.'

'Thanks, Martin.' Sarah rinsed her cup and then smiled. 'I'll need a few weeks just to finish all the paperwork you've given me.'

Martin frowned. 'That reminds me, I've given Angela a large stack of results that need tabling for the paper on the effects of low-dose medication on preventing recurrence of febrile seizures. I'd really like to get it away this month. Would you like me to take over the writing?'

'And lose first authorship? No way.' Sarah shook back her hair. 'I'll manage.'

They walked out of the kitchen together. Sarah

had passed on the decision of whether to discharge Anthony by the time they reached the office. Angela waved a result form at Sarah.

'First bloods back on Charlotte Newman. Looks like you were right, Sarah.'

'What about?' enquired Martin.

'Case of meningococcal meningitis,' Sarah informed him. 'I'm just going to review her now.'

'I'll come with you.' The consultant turned to Angela. 'Can you restrain young Anthony, please? I'll examine him with a view to discharge in a few minutes.'

Sarah caught Angela's expression and smiled. Another good outcome likely. All things considered, it had really been quite an extraordinary day.

When her beeper later heralded a call from Paul Henderson, confirming their dinner arrangement, Sarah had to take a deep breath and remind herself that the day was not yet over.

Only a year ago the muted decor and peaceful solitude of the small, high-rise apartment had seemed a haven. Now it was little short of being oppressive. Sarah dropped her large canvas shoulder-bag onto the oversized cream sofa as she hurried past. Several journals, pens, a floppy disk and the sheaf of lab results that needed tabling slid out to land on the pale pink carpet. Sarah ignored them.

Stepping out of the shower a few minutes later, Sarah wrapped a towel around her hair and bypassed the pile of clothes on the floor. Then she sighed, turned and scooped up the pile, depositing it firmly in the laundry basket. Catching sight of her

sweatshirt, Sarah shook her head. Bart Simpson
clothing and a Mickey Mouse hat. Well, that was
an impression she had every intention of blotting
out.

Easing on the sheer black tights that completed
a set of sensuous lingerie, Sarah was aware of the
knot of excitement centred a little lower than her
stomach—excitement that Sarah Kendall had not
associated with a man for many years. Her career
had always been her priority. Was it just because
she was feeling dissatisfied with the direction her
life was taking that she was feeling this way now?
Or was it just that she had finally met a man whose
attractions she couldn't resist?

'It's purely an intellectual attraction,' she told
herself as she chose the most sophisticated dress she
could find in her wardrobe. Slipping on the sleek-
fitting, black short-sleeved dress, Sarah was delighted to find it was still a perfect fit. Goodness
knows how long it was since she had last worn it.
She added a string of tiny pearls to follow the curve
of the rounded neckline.

Armed with a hair-dryer, Sarah swept her over-
long fringe out of her eyes and turned the ends of
her hair under so that it hung just above her shoulders and swung in a smooth curtain when she
moved her head. Hurriedly, she redid her make-up,
put in some pearl stud earrings and eased her feet
into the black high-heeled court shoes. At five feet-
six she had no need of the extra height and no doubt
her arches would not be thanking her later, but
Sarah was determined to present an ultimately fem-
inine image.

Simply tactics, she reasoned. It was Paul, after all, who had described their opposing views as a war zone. After this morning he was hardly likely to expect sophistication. Throwing his expectations off balance could only be to her advantage. In fact, it was surprising that he hadn't suggested meeting at the Pizza Hut or McDonald's instead of the up-market French restaurant they had agreed on. Sarah grabbed a light evening jacket and bag and quickly locked up her apartment. Another advantage might be to arrive at the restaurant a few minutes early.

Sarah did arrive early at the restaurant but not as early as Paul. He got to his feet lazily as the waiter showed Sarah to the quiet corner table, his dinner jacket and immaculate grooming as appropriate to the elegant setting as her own attire. But Paul Henderson had gone one better. As the musky scent of his aftershave greeted Sarah's appreciative nostrils she realised she had completely forgotten to apply any perfume. She cursed inwardly even as she smilingly accepted the proffered glass of champagne.

'How did you know I liked champagne, Mr Henderson?'

'I didn't.' He cocked an eyebrow. 'I thought you might like something to argue about—to break the ice, as it were.' The smile was teasing. 'Ordering something, without letting you have your say, seemed like an ideal way to accomplish it. *Dr Kendall*,' Paul added, the emphasis on her title tempered by what Sarah now realised was a rather charming smile.

'You can call me Sarah,' she offered, returning the smile. 'Actually, I love champagne.'

Paul raised his glass in a toast and Sarah drew in a long breath as the crystal clinked musically. Ice might be more appropriate than anything to break it with, she thought with dismay. The room must be over-heated. That was a far more acceptable reason for the increased heart rate and flushed skin Sarah was experiencing than the effect of a man she had met only hours previously.

'It's rather warm in here, don't you think?'

'Just right for me.'

The steady gaze of the dark blue eyes made Sarah uncomfortably suspicious that Paul knew exactly how she was feeling—and the real reason why. She shook back her hair.

'I'm surprised. Isn't being cold-blooded a prerequisite for a position in management? I would expect you to be more affected by heat.'

'We thrive on it.' Paul leaned across the table. 'In fact, we need a certain amount to even get moving. We lie about in our offices, just hoping that some hot-blooded medico is going to come storming in and generate enough heat to stimulate some action.'

Sarah laughed. Her contagious gurgle was enough to make heads turn at a neighbouring table, smiling in response to the sound.

'I suppose I ought to apologise.'

'Please don't.' Paul drew the champagne bottle from its nest of ice in the silver bucket. 'It's not often that an incredibly attractive and incredibly angry woman bursts into my office and rants at me on someone else's behalf.'

Sarah held up her glass as he spoke and Paul put the neck of the bottle to its rim. The glass shook slightly and Paul's other hand closed over Sarah's to hold it steady. The hiss of escaping bubbles was not masked by Paul's soft words.

'It could be the most exciting thing that's ever happened to me.'

The glass was full but Paul did not release either her hand or her gaze. Sarah swallowed hard.

'I wasn't going to.'

'Burst in?'

'No—apologise.'

Paul's laughter broke the increasing tension the touch of their hands had evoked. Sarah concentrated hard not to spill her wine as he finally released her hand.

'The end justifies the means, I take it?' His smile was again teasing.

'In this case, absolutely.'

Paul looked around as the three-piece band started some unobtrusive, romantic background music.

'Do you dance, Dr Kendall?'

'Not often, Mr Henderson. Do you?'

'Almost never.' He held her gaze. 'Shall we?'

'Why not?'

Sarah found she could think of several reasons the instant Paul Henderson's hands touched her body. The air around them seemed alive with a sexual tension she found frightening. She had only just met the man, for heaven's sake, but her feelings

were so powerful she felt she would betray them if
she relaxed even slightly. They moved awkwardly,
out of time to the music, and both seemed relieved
to break off and return to their table where they
spent several minutes in silence, studying and making selections from the menu.

The silence continued. And grew. By the time
their entrées were served it was decidedly uncom-
fortable. Sarah found it unbearable but couldn't
think of a way to break it. Paul seemed nervous.
Even though she knew virtually nothing about the
man, sitting opposite her, Sarah sensed that his
nerves were completely out of character. They both
ignored the food on the table. Sarah was reaching
down beside her chair for her evening bag, on the
point of excusing herself to visit the rest-room,
when Paul suddenly cleared his throat.

'Do you believe in love at first sight, Sarah
Kendall?'

Sarah dropped the bag. 'No,' she responded
quickly. Then her eyes met the intense stare directed at her. She felt drawn into the gaze as though
by a magnetic force. She was enveloped in it, cap-
tured by its intensity and the answering response
she felt to it. Her voice was now a whisper. 'That
is, I never thought…' The whisper faded.

'I would have said no as well—' Paul filled the
silence quickly '—yesterday. Now I'm not so sure.'
He frowned slightly. 'I'm not talking about sexual
attraction, here, Sarah—however powerful I recognise that can be. I'm talking about something
more…' He searched for the word he wanted.
'More profound.' Paul leaned across the small table

again. 'I find you profoundly disturbing, Dr Sarah Kendall.'

Sarah laughed nervously. 'Gee, thanks,' she quipped. Then she sobered. She knew it had been a struggle for Paul to say what he had. To reveal his feelings on such a personal level. Suddenly she was in a position of power over a man she had met only that morning—one she had seen only as a powerful adversary. The power she had now been handed was on a different level, certainly, but it was no less real and its significance was frightening.

'I don't claim to be intuitive,' Paul said quietly, 'and I don't think I'm entirely egotistical, but it seems to me there's something a little unusual happening here. Either what I'm feeling is being simply reflected back at me or there's a possibility that you're experiencing something similar.' His look held an apology. 'Perhaps I'm making a fool of myself. You can tell me if I am. I can take it.' His mouth curved into a half-smile. 'It's another prerequisite of being a manager.'

This was crazy, Sarah thought. She was caught in an emotional tidal wave which reason told her was simply not possible. Yet it was happening, and part of her had no desire to fight it. A large part of her.

'You're not making a fool of yourself, Paul,' she finally answered a little shakily. 'But it's too fast— too big. It's frightening. We don't even know each other.'

'Sarah Margaret Kendall, age thirty-three. Majored in education and child psychology, gaining a double degree with distinction before entering medical school, from which graduation was also with distinction. Reports from all specialties worked in are outstanding, particularly Paediatrics, the current run in which is due to expire next month.

'The only reservation held by consultants is that Sarah Kendall is inclined to become too emotionally involved with her case-load. She is highly recommended for a consultancy position if applied for but the impression given is that she may wish to proceed in another direction. Sarah Kendall is, for some inexplicable reason, single, lives alone and is quite probably the most beautiful woman on earth.'

Sarah grinned. 'You didn't get that last bit off my file.' She sat back, feeling the tension ease a little. 'OK. Fair's fair. Where do I get the file on you?'

Paul's smile was calculating. 'Perhaps I should retain a certain air of mystery. It might make me more attractive.'

'I wouldn't worry about that,' Sarah muttered darkly.

'Suits me.' The smile became almost smug. 'What is it you'd like to know?'

Sarah's query was prevented by the arrival of an unhappy-looking waiter.

'There is something wrong with your soup? Sir? Madam?'

Sarah and Paul looked at each other guiltily. They had completely forgotten their entrées.

'I'm sorry,' Paul said smoothly. 'There is nothing wrong with the soup. We were—ah—distracted.' He caught Sarah's eye again and they both suppressed smiles.

'I understand, sir.' The waiter's eyebrows moved fractionally. 'Would you like some more soup or shall I serve your main course?'

'The main course, thank you,' Paul responded. 'I don't think either of us really needs an entrée, do we, Sarah?'

The double meaning may have been lost on the waiter but Sarah understood only too well. She swallowed hard. The birth of their relationship had been fiery. It had already escalated into what, for Sarah, was unknown territory. Should she simply allow it to happen? And what would happen? A tumultuous ending perhaps with scars on both sides? Or was the bridled passion something that could grow and eclipse the shadows of the unknown? That possibility was too important to compromise.

'No,' Sarah agreed quietly. 'We don't need an entrée.'

CHAPTER THREE

THE outpatient visit had been more for the mother's benefit than the child's.

Having dispensed explanations and reassurance over the period of what had become a lengthy visit, Sarah had to force herself to concentrate on her task. The odd but very pleasurable tingle that announced her mind was slipping back to last night's dinner—or, rather, what had happened afterwards—simply had to be overruled.

'I've checked Chelsea over very carefully, Mrs Ross,' Sarah announced. 'There's no evidence of any physical abnormality or developmental problems. Basically, she's a very healthy little girl. The fact that she's had febrile convulsions doesn't necessarily mean that she's epileptic.'

'But she's had two!' Mrs Ross said for the third time. 'And one of them was that horrible long one. It went on for hours! I was so sure she was going to die!'

'Prolonged seizures are very distressing. Even the twenty minutes or so that Chelsea suffered can seem much longer. Most of them are, however, a child's first febrile convulsion, as it was in Chelsea's case. The risk of recurrence of prolonged episodes is very low, about one to four per cent. They are far more likely to last only thirty seconds to a few minutes as Chelsea's recent convulsion did.'

Mrs Ross wasn't convinced and shook her head in disbelief. Sarah sighed inwardly.

'Chelsea hasn't suffered more than one convulsion during each period she has been running a high temperature. She was admitted to hospital after her first seizure and the investigations were very thorough. We have, in fact, just completed a study that suggests low-dose medication has no effect on the possible recurrence of seizures. When you move to higher doses you get into problems with side-effects. You have no family history of epilepsy and there is no evidence of any abnormal development. I don't feel there is an indication at present that Chelsea should be on long-term, continuous medication.

'As I said, we'll give you some diazepam suppositories which can be used in the unlikely event that Chelsea has another seizure lasting more than five minutes. Are you sure you understand what I told you about their administration?'

Mrs Ross nodded. She looked a little happier at being reminded of the emergency medication.

'If that should happen then certainly we would look at continuous medication, but in the meantime you can take measures to help prevent this happening again, Mrs Ross.' Sarah spoke encouragingly. 'If you have any suspicion that Chelsea is running a fever then take her temperature. If it's up at all give her some paracetamol, remove any warm clothing and sponge her down with a damp cloth. Don't use cold water or fans, though, because that will make her shiver and actually raise her temperature. It's not a guarantee to prevent recurrence but it can certainly help.'

Sarah glanced over at the toddler who was happily sifting through the basket of toys in the corner of the examination room. She knew there was a waiting room full of people outside and she was desperate for a cup of coffee after this, her third case of the clinic.

'We'll review Chelsea in three months, Mrs Ross, unless there's a problem, of course. Your GP can contact us at any time.' Sarah stood up, signalling an end to the interview. She handed over the prescription she had written, whilst talking. 'I'm confident you won't need to use this but having it available should certainly help your peace of mind.'

The outpatients' senior nurse came in as Mrs Ross left with her daughter. She handed Sarah a cup of coffee.

'You've got two minutes till I send in the next one,' she warned. 'Let's hope they're not all as anxious as Mrs Ross!'

Two minutes. Sarah closed her eyes and blissfully let her mind escape back in time. What an amazing evening! That second dance they'd had before their main course had been served... Suddenly their bodies had melded together as one fluid unit with not a hint of the earlier stilted movement. The main course had arrived, and had been ignored. The chef had been the one to enquire what was wrong at that point. Both too inebriated with emotion to be embarrassed, Paul and Sarah had paid the bill and escaped the restaurant.

Whose idea had it been that they went back to her apartment? Sarah couldn't remember. The pleasurable tingle became almost pain as Sarah relived the next part of the evening. If their bodies had melded together on the dance floor so well, it had been a pale shadow of the union of their love-making.

'Oh, God!' Sarah groaned, feeling herself blush furiously. 'On a first date, too!'

Never in her life had she allowed things to happen at such an extraordinary pace but, then, she had never in her life felt this way about anyone else. It had seemed so wrong but at the same time so absolutely right. It had only been during the drowsy peace of spent passion that Sarah had realised she still knew nothing about this man. And she hadn't had the chance to talk then.

Paul's departure from her bed and her apartment had been distressingly abrupt. His reasoning that he couldn't turn up at work in his dinner jacket hadn't really excused his haste, but his final lengthy kiss and whispered words had.

'I may have only met you for the first time this morning, Sarah Kendall, but I feel like I've known you in my heart for a very long time.'

The kiss had stifled any reply but Sarah could only have agreed. It had to be some sort of magic and, as such, Sarah suspected it could vanish as quickly as it had appeared. Even if it did, she could never regret having experienced it. It was more than falling in love. It was—

It was young Lawrence West, a child who was failing to thrive and suffered from recurrent respiratory infections. He was going to need comprehensive examination and investigation for the possibility of cystic fibrosis. Sarah could only hope that her consultant was moving his share of the patient load through at a faster pace, otherwise they would have no hope of finishing this clinic by lunchtime.

In fact, it was one o'clock by the time Sarah headed in the direction of Ward 23. She had a date with another young boy and a pair of crutches, which she had no intention of missing for anybody.

Well, almost anybody. Seeing Paul striding towards her in the busy main floor corridor, Sarah's step faltered and her skin flushed with confusion. How could they act normally after last night? What if he thought that was a typical first date on her part? Confusion was replaced by embarrassment and Sarah concluded that attack had to be the best form of defence.

'So, you did make it in eventually.'

'What do you mean?' Paul came to a halt, standing very close to her. Sarah didn't move back.

'I went up to your office at 8 a.m. I was dropping in Alice Forster's notes. You said you wanted to look at them in case of legal repercussions?'

Paul nodded. 'I got them. Thanks.'

'Well, your secretary tells me you're never in before nine.'

He nodded again. 'Is that a problem?'

Sarah laughed. 'Not at all. Nice work if you can get it!'

'Too right.' Paul leaned even closer. 'I think I'm going to have to kiss you. Right now.'

'No way!' Sarah took a step back and glanced

nervously over her shoulder. 'I have to go. I have
a very important appointment.'

'What are you doing tonight?'

Sarah's pulse rate zoomed up as she caught the
look of desire in those amazingly blue eyes. It cor-
responded with a distinct thump in the region of her
lower abdomen. She knew what she'd like to be
doing tonight.

'I'm on call,' she said sadly. 'Neonatal Intensive
Care. I'll be here all night.'

Paul smiled at her tone. 'Never mind,' he con-
soled her. 'There'll be another time.'

'You bet,' Sarah said. 'And not just for what
you're thinking about, Paul Henderson. I still know
absolutely nothing about you.'

Paul's eyebrows lifted suggestively but Sarah ignored the innuendo and began to move away.

'And what's more, I haven't even begun to give
you my views on hospital management.'

Paul's smile was decidedly smug, Sarah thought.
Once again he had the upper hand. Why was it that
Sarah felt he was so completely in control of this
situation? That he was creating the magic that had
her caught so completely in its spell?

Angela waved at Sarah as she hurried through the
ward.

'I was just going to beep you. Michael's been
waiting there for ten minutes. He won't even sit
down. Here...' Angela reached into the store cupboard and produced the adult-sized pair of crutches.
'And try not to make too much noise, please. It is
rest time.'

Sarah grinned. She knew Angela was just as thrilled as she was at the breakthrough with Michael. They were, however, much quieter today. Sarah tucked one leg up behind her and hopped beside the boy who made a valiant effort, despite tiring halfway down the corridor. She deliberately made her own effort even more awkward.

'You cheated again,' he accused her. 'You let me win.'

'You deserved to,' Sarah told him. 'It was much harder work for you.' She gave him a hug. 'Well done, Michael. I'm proud of you.'

He looked mollified. 'I'll get faster,' he stated. 'I just need more practice.'

'Absolutely,' Sarah agreed. 'But have lots of rests too, though. Same time tomorrow?'

'Yeah, I guess.'

Alice wasn't asleep this afternoon. She lay in her mother's arms, the blue shadowing under her eyes indicating a bad spell. Sarah kissed her gently.

'Seen any ducks today, darling?'

Alice nodded slowly. 'Six,' she whispered. 'But no ducklings yet.'

'Maybe tomorrow.' Sarah smiled. She caught Isobel's eye. They both knew it was the wrong time of year for ducklings but it was too hard not to allow Alice some hope of a fervent wish. Isobel's eyes were also heavily shadowed.

'Bad night?' Sarah queried unnecessarily. At Isobel's nod she pressed her lips together thoughtfully. 'We might need to increase the morphine dose in the infusion and make it continuous,' she said quietly, stroking the bald head of the child in Isobel's arms. 'Where is it hurting, sweetheart? Is it your legs again?'

'It was my tummy,' Alice said, 'but it's better now.' She closed her eyes, easing her head back onto her mother's shoulder.

Sarah waited until Alice was asleep, before discussing the potential bowel and bladder problems her young patient might be facing due to her degree of debility and the pain relief she needed. They both agreed that any invasive procedures had to be avoided unless the problems became unbearable. Sarah charted a very mild laxative when she returned to the ward office. Her familiar sadness at the Forsters' situation was increased, if anything, today by the personal happiness that had burst into her own life.

It was because of Alice Forster that this has happened, she realised suddenly. Would it be too much to expect a little of the magic to rub off on her?

The stress of the neonatal intensive care unit was particularly noticeable that evening—so many tiny scraps of humanity, fighting the odds for survival, a few disbelieving parents, keeping a late vigil by the incubators. Sarah hated to see the impossibly small babies on life support systems, attached by so many wires and tubes to the ventilators and monitoring systems. She recognised that she felt it too keenly. While she knew her performance was still better than average in this area she also knew that it wasn't a place she wanted to be in the long term.

What did she want long term? Sarah loved her

work with children, loved the interaction with their families. But it wasn't enough. With each discharge she felt a loss, a termination of her care which seemed unsatisfying. If she was lucky she might see them again in an outpatient clinic but more often than not they simply vanished from her life. There were plenty more to take their place, of course, but the overall effect was draining. Sarah knew she gave too much. She made repeated efforts to keep her involvement purely professional, but then an Alice Forster or a Michael came along and she was lost again.

There was the research as well, and Sarah loved the academic side to her job. There was immense satisfaction to be gained by collecting, analysing and forming conclusions about data that might be of direct benefit to others. Even the writing was satisfying when she finally found the time to do it. Writing a textbook was another attractive possibility, but on its own it would still be not enough.

Sarah Kendall was searching for a focus in her life. It was what made her reaction to meeting Paul Henderson so frightening. The thought that she may have found something which she had unknowingly been searching for wasn't something she was ready to admit, even to herself, because she couldn't know whether it was to be trusted. To know that it was so central to her life and then to lose it would be far worse than not knowing.

She could admit to sexual attraction, the passion she had never known she was capable of. She could admit to being in love. That was reasonable even given the short time frame. What wasn't reasonable was to suggest that it could be the core of her future happiness and satisfaction with life. That was simply too dangerous to be reasonable.

The nagging feeling that the significance of this new relationship was too great added an underlying stress level that her evening's work only increased. When her beeper went again shortly after 9 p.m. Sarah felt bone weary and her tone was dispirited when she punched the buttons for the telephone number her pager displayed. It was not a number she recognised.

'Sarah Kendall.'

'I love you, Sarah.'

It was the last thing Sarah had expected to hear, and her weariness evaporated instantly. Excitement took its place.

'Hello, Paul. Where are you?' The call had been internal.

'In my office. We had an emergency meeting thanks to this threatened strike by the cleaners. Can I buy you a coffee?'

'Actually, I'd love some fresh air. I'll meet you in the courtyard in front of your block.'

The crisp night air was refreshing but any chill Sarah experienced was negated by the warmth of Paul's body as he took her in his arms. His lips met hers with a gentle greeting that quickly spiralled into a reminder of last night's passion. Sarah responded avidly to the silken caress of his tongue and lips, needing no encouragement to press the length of her body against his. Paul's desire was obvious but Sarah knew it couldn't be any greater than her own. It took a supreme effort to push herself away.

'This isn't the place for this, Paul.'

His grin was wicked. 'Come up to my office, then.'

'I'm on call,' Sarah reminded him. Not that the idea wasn't tempting. She stepped further away from Paul to try and distract herself, moving to sit on a bench set amongst the shrubbery. 'Come and talk to me instead.'

Paul sat willingly beside her and took hold of her hand.

'So, how's it going, Dr Kendall?'

'Awful,' Sarah replied despondently. 'We just had a premature delivery of twins. We had to ventilate both of them due to severe respiratory distress syndrome. The anaesthetist took care of one but I had to do the other. It's a procedure I really hate.'

'Endotracheal or nasotracheal intubation?'

'Nasotracheal. They looked like they might need ventilation for quite a while.'

'What gestation?'

'Twenty-eight weeks—but they were really tiny. Eleven hundred and nine hundred grams.'

'Still, survival is more directly linked to maturity than weight, isn't it? What were their five-minute Apgar scores like?' Paul stopped suddenly. 'Why are you staring at me like that, Sarah?'

'You're a manager, Paul Henderson.' Sarah spoke very slowly. 'Why do I feel like I'm talking to another doctor?'

Paul smiled. He looked, Sarah thought, as though he were about to pull a rabbit from a hat.

'I was a general surgeon in my previous life,' he admitted. 'Smallish hospital. I had a few emergency Caesareans to handle.'

Sarah kept staring. 'Just how previous was this life?'

'I've been in management for three years now. I've done the odd locum, just to keep my hand in. I miss the patient contact.'

Sarah let her breath out in a silent whistle. If anything, this admission underlined the fact that she knew nothing about this man. What on earth would send a surgeon into the management camp? A career disaster of some kind? Being struck off? No, he couldn't have been struck off if he'd been doing locums. Disturbed, Sarah withdrew her hand from Paul's.

'What made you go into management?'

'Various things,' Paul replied. He seemed suddenly preoccupied.

'Don't be evasive,' Sarah said, more sharply than she'd intended. 'I need to know what your motivation was. It just seems such an extraordinary thing to do.'

Paul rubbed his chin with his hand. 'OK. I was working in a small hospital. I could see the problems with the health system the way it was—we all could. Waiting lists increasing, operating time being cut, good staff leaving in droves to enter the private system or go overseas. I could see the need for reform, I could see what management was trying to achieve and I could see only too clearly the huge gap in comprehension and communication between management and medical staff. I thought there had to be a way to bridge the gap. I thought I could do it. When the opportunity came up for a management position I took it.'

Sarah nodded. So far it seemed a plausible motivation. Admirable, even.

'I was a great success,' Paul continued with a modest smile. 'We stayed within budget, cut waiting lists and improved standards of patient care and working conditions. After some initial hiccups relations between management and medical staff improved dramatically.'

'You proved your point, then,' Sarah said, 'so why didn't you go back to practising medicine? You said you missed the patient contact.'

'I was head-hunted. If it worked in a small hospital, why not try it on a much larger scale? Besides...' He grinned at Sarah. 'What medical position would allow me to roll in at 9 a.m., have weekends off and no call?'

'You're not at home now,' Sarah reminded him. She glanced at Paul curiously. 'Is it working on a larger scale, then?'

Paul shrugged. 'No. Not yet. The system is too fragmented. There's too much antagonism and resistance to change. And I'm getting bogged down with things like this cleaners' dispute.'

'What's the problem?'

'We have a small pool of permanent staff who put in a lot of overtime. It would be far more cost effective to employ more people on a standard rate of pay. It would also improve the service. Amongst other changes to working conditions the union won't agree to its members losing the overtime bonuses. I can see both sides of the issue but I can't allow it to jeopardise the efficient running of the hospital and it seems so far away from the medical issues I'd rather be involved in.' He caught Sarah's hand again. 'Then someone like you bursts into my office and I suddenly realise how far away I am from real hands-on medicine.'

'You sound unhappy with your job.'

'I am. I know I haven't been here long but I feel caught in no man's land between each side in a war zone. I'm failing both sides and can't see a way to bring them closer. I'm frustrated, I guess. I'm not sure this is the direction I want my career to take. I'm forty years old now, Sarah. I feel I ought to know which way I'm going by now and be happy with it.'

'I know the feeing,' Sarah murmured. She squeezed the hand holding hers. So many questions were now tumbling through her head. She had made a start in understanding Paul but there was so much more she wanted to know. While his explanation of his career change was plausible Sarah instinctively felt there was more to it. As she framed her next query, however, her beeper sounded.

'Damn,' she muttered. 'Just when I'm finally finding out something about you.' She unclipped her pager.

'There's always next time.' Paul smiled. 'That will be your turn to rave on. What are you doing tomorrow night?'

'It's my mother's birthday. Family party,' Sarah said apologetically. 'What about the weekend?'

'I'm tied up, I'm afraid.' Paul also looked apologetic.

'The whole weekend?' Sarah's eyes widened with surprise.

'Afraid so.'

Sarah glanced at her pager as it beeped again. 'That's the emergency department,' she said quickly. 'I'll have to run.'

And run she did. It wasn't far from the courtyard but it gave Sarah time to wonder at what now seemed like evasiveness on Paul's part. The whole weekend? He hadn't even offered any sort of explanation. He was hiding something, Sarah concluded, just like he'd hidden the fact he was a doctor. Man of mystery, indeed. Just how much could she trust him?

He rang her three times during the next day, but trying to see each other proved to be an exercise in frustration. Paul was caught all morning in further meetings with the cleaners' union. Lunch was out. Sarah had managed to finalise her presentation for the paediatricians' meeting between calls last night. Now she had to deliver it. Sarah missed the planned coffee together mid-afternoon due to the admission of three-year-old Amy Turner who was suffering what appeared to be a severe dose of measles. It had upset ward routine. The case needed to be isolated, immunisation details checked on other patients and the worry discussed that the epidemic being experienced up north was making an appearance in the South Island. Sarah rang Paul's office just after five to find he'd already left for the day.

'Nice for some,' she muttered darkly. She realised that, among many other things, she had absolutely no idea where Paul lived or what his home telephone number was. Still, a little breathing space over the weekend was probably a very good thing. She might even be able to view recent events in a more objective light.

'It has to be a man!' The delighted repetition by her older sister, Helen, grated on Sarah.

'Nonsense. Why can't I just look happy to be having an evening at home? It is Mum's birthday after all.' Sarah bent to scratch the ears of an elderly golden retriever, who waved his tail gently in appreciation.

'It's more than that.' Helen peered closely at her sister. 'You look like...' She paused to consider, her lips pursed. 'You look like a woman who's recently had a very good—' She whispered the last of her sentence into Sarah's ear.

Sarah looked shocked. 'Helen!' She glanced at the door as her nine-year-old niece, Holly, bounded into the room, flanked by two more retrievers. 'Shh!' she warned Helen.

'Well, it's about time—that's all I can say.' Helen reached for a box of matches. 'Holly, do you want to help me light the candles?'

Sarah paused in the doorway of the dining room while the cake was being carried triumphantly to the table. She gazed at her parents with great affection. Her father, Jack, was a country GP, a large, gentle man who took his job and position in the small rural community very seriously. Her mother,

Evelyn, was also a large woman, her size matched by her cheerful and enthusiastic personality. Evelyn had also trained as a doctor but had given up her career without apparent regret to raise her three children.

The eldest, John, lived in Australia. Helen had become a solo mother when Holly's father had walked out on them shortly after her birth. Now that Sarah had also left home Evelyn devoted her considerable energies to her beloved dogs. She bred and trained retrievers, often travelling to show them or to compete in obedience or agility trials.

Sarah joined in the singing, kissed her mother, declined the cake and with some difficulty moved the rumps of two dogs to allow room for her to sit on the huge old sofa. Watching her mother open and exclaim over her gifts with Holly's enthusiastic input, Sarah relaxed and soaked in the atmosphere. She loved this place.

The rambling country house was never quite tidy, always smelled of dogs and was one of the happiest places Sarah knew. It was a home in every sense of the word, and Sarah missed belonging here the way she used to. She would always feel at home and be welcomed here but it wasn't the same any more. It wasn't enough.

Her sterile apartment only accentuated what she was missing but even a house in the country wouldn't be a solution. It was the whole package Sarah craved. Home—and family. And career, she reminded herself. Perhaps her mother's example had put her off even looking up till now. She had loved her career too much to even consider its sacrifice, despite her mother's declaration that motherhood was the ultimate career.

It certainly wasn't that she was missing interaction with children. Quite apart from her work, Sarah was almost a second mother to Holly and had shared as much as possible of her upbringing so far. She welcomed the girl now with a big hug as Holly came over to share the sofa. Carrying dishes away from the table, Helen paused to smile at their embrace.

'Tick, tick,' she said cheerfully to Sarah.

'What?'

'It's your biological clock. I can hear it from here!'

Sarah groaned and disentangled herself from the squash of child and dogs to help clear the table. Children were certainly part of the nebulous package she wanted her future to contain. Children, a dog or two, of course, and...a husband. Helen might declare that they were entirely superfluous but her bitterness belied her conviction. Sarah had observed her struggles as a single mother and knew it wasn't an option she would choose either. Thank goodness she had been practical enough to unearth some protection from the depths of her bathroom cupboard the other night.

The hour's drive back to the city later that evening gave Sarah too much time to think. She had spent considerable energy recently, wondering where her career was heading. Now her desires seemed to be crystallising with an entirely new priority. Was it the frustration with pressures at work? An overload of emotional involvement with cases that either ended in tragedy or vanished from her life? Or was it because up until now a vital piece of the jigsaw had been missing?

Was Paul Henderson the missing piece?

The Saturday morning ward round went quickly. Alice Forster had rallied, her pain well controlled again. Isobel took her out in a wheelchair to feed the ducks and get some sunshine. Michael was practising hard with his crutches but Sarah wasn't quite ready to discharge him.

'Maybe on Monday,' she promised. 'I've got one more challenge for you first.'

Charlotte Newman was well on the way to recovery, her temperature normal for the first time. Another forty-eight hours and she could also go home.

All in all, it was a satisfying morning and Sarah decided she would spend the rest of the day working on her paper. She had nothing better to do unfortunately. Feeling disturbed at the sudden dip in the emotional roller coaster the last few days had provided, Sarah stopped in the main foyer of the hospital on her way out. A chocolate bar from the vending machine was definitely called for.

It was while she was searching for some coins in her wallet that Sarah became aware of the boy sitting in the waiting area on the other side of the foyer. Although she could only see the back of his dark head, something about him alerted Sarah that he was doing something he knew he shouldn't.

Intrigued, she fished her chocolate bar out of the dispensing hatch and moved towards the boy. He reminded her of Michael. Perhaps it was just the fact that he was sitting alone. Or maybe it was the slump of the skinny shoulders. She still couldn't see what he was doing. Breaking off a piece of chocolate, Sarah bit into it and edged closer. Then she smiled.

The boy was carefully and very furtively ripping a page out of one of the magazines left for people in the waiting area. He had it mostly covered with his hand as he slowly removed it, glancing around frequently to check whether he was being observed. He hadn't noticed Sarah, approaching from behind. Once removed, he quickly folded and refolded the picture, but not before Sarah had glimpsed it—a police officer, holding his dog. The huge German shepherd was smiling more than his handler, Sarah thought. She moved closer to the boy.

'Hi, there,' she said cheerfully. 'You're not lost, are you?'

The boy jumped guiltily and stuffed the picture into his pocket. He shot a quick glance at Sarah but she ignored his action.

'Would you like a piece of chocolate?'

The look she now received told Sarah that no one was stupid enough to talk to, let alone accept a gift from, a stranger. Sarah was struck by her second glimpse of the child's eyes. A very dark blue. He reminded her strongly of someone but she wasn't so sure it was Michael any more.

'My name's Sarah,' she offered, sitting beside him. She wasn't happy, leaving him to wait on his own. The boy's shoulders hunched a little further and Sarah received no reply. She tried again.

'What's your name?'

'Daniel.'

But it wasn't the boy who spoke. At the now familiar tingle the voice caused, Sarah looked up, startled. She looked up at the tall figure of Paul Henderson, at the dark eyes now observing her very carefully. And suddenly, appallingly, she knew who this child reminded her so strongly of. He was a junior version of the man standing in front of her.

'His name's Daniel,' Paul said. 'He's my son.'

Sarah's mouth dropped open. She scrambled to her feet. She could feel the blood drain from her face. Of course. It all made sense. She'd known he'd been hiding something. She'd known there was reason to doubt whether she could give her trust as easily as she had given her body to this man. She clenched her fists.

'I can see what ties up your weekends,' Sarah said tightly. 'It's an important family time.'

'Yes, it is,' Paul agreed evenly. 'We're going fishing this afternoon.'

'I'm sure you'll catch something,' Sarah said flatly. Her horror was being overtaken by anger— an anger even greater than that which had first propelled her into Paul Henderson's orbit. She lowered her voice to an acid whisper. 'I'm sure you can hook anything you fancy.'

Sarah turned and fled as fast as dignity in a public place would allow, but not fast enough. Paul caught her arm and pulled her to a halt beside the vending machine.

'Just what did you mean by that remark?' His voice was quiet. Dangerously quiet.

Sarah jerked her arm free, rubbing it with unnecessary vigour.

'You must think I'm really stupid, Paul. Either that or you're so full of yourself it didn't occur to you to think it might matter.' She kept rubbing her arm. It had hurt, but not that much. 'I understand now why it was so urgent for you to get home the other night. Management meetings don't usually go through to breakfast, do they?' Sarah laughed incredulously. 'How long did you think it would take for me to find out, Paul?'

'I was going to tell you—'

'Like hell you were!' Sarah snarled. She ignored the startled look from a man who was approaching the vending machine. The stranger changed his mind and walked away rapidly.

'It was a good line, Paul. ''Do you believe in love at first sight?''' Sarah's mimicking was sarcastic. 'Do you often use it, Paul? Does it always work that quickly when you fancy a bit on the side?'

The anger flashed in Paul's eyes. 'You surprise me, Dr Kendall. Perhaps you're not the person I thought you were.'

'Obviously not,' Sarah agreed venomously. 'You don't know me at all, Paul Henderson.'

'And you don't know me.' The clipped tone was a warning.

'I don't think I want to,' Sarah said slowly. She glanced over at Daniel who was watching them, his face expressionless. Sarah turned away. It felt as if time was suddenly in slow motion.

'Your son is waiting for you. Goodbye, Paul.'

CHAPTER FOUR

THERE wasn't much satisfaction to be gained by saying 'I told you so' to herself, but Sarah said it anyway.

How right she had been to suspect that Paul was hiding something. How naïve was it possible to be at the age of thirty-three? He was forty years old. No woman in her right mind would bother denying how good-looking he was, an ex-surgeon who now had a job in senior management with, she imagined, an executive salary to boot. Of course he would be married. And what woman could be married to Paul Henderson, without wanting to produce a junior Paul or Paula? Probably a couple of each, Sarah told herself bitterly.

How right she had also been not to allow herself to give in to the idea that his significance in her future might be paramount. Missing piece of the jigsaw, indeed. Huh! Perhaps Helen was right, after all, in her assertion that men were simply not worth the trouble.

Why could she find absolutely no satisfaction in proving herself so right? It was as though a door she had been undecided about trying had now been slammed and locked in her face, thereby removing the choice she had wanted the chance to make. Well, so be it, then. She had a wonderful career and more children than she could cope with. She would simply have to make the best of it. She just wished her traitorous body would co-operate and stop preventing sleep by the painfully vivid memories of the sensations those skilled hands could arouse...

It was amazing how constructive anger could be when channelled in the right direction. The paper on the use of low-dose medication to prevent recurrences of febrile seizures fell into place and was written with remarkable speed and cohesion. Sarah knew her conclusions, which contradicted recent reports from other groups, would spark some controversy but she also knew that they were soundly based.

It was to be hoped that they might spur other research teams to expand their own investigations, thereby improving knowledge on dosages and regimes that would provide the most effective therapy. Delivering the paper to Martin Lynch's secretary on Monday morning to be typed up, Sarah then swung her attention towards her patients. There was no medical problem that could be thrown at her at present that she couldn't handle. The more the merrier.

There was certainly more but none were particularly merry. Two more cases of measles had been admitted over the weekend. The case she had admitted on Friday afternoon was causing concern and had been seen due to severe conjunctivitis and emergent bronchitis the previous day. The complication of pneumonia was a real danger with measles and antibiotics had been started. Sarah was even more concerned when told that Amy Turner had been difficult to wake that morning.

Post-infectious encephalomyelitis was a very serious complication of measles and carried a high mortality rate of ten per cent. The toddler was Sarah's first port of call.

Amy's pulse rate was slow and her breathing slightly irregular, but what was more alarming were the unequal pupil sizes and abnormal reflexes on one side. Sarah called in Martin Lynch immediately. After his examination he called the paediatric intensive care specialist and they arranged an urgent CT scan to check for raised intracranial pressure. They also arranged transfer of the child to the intensive care unit.

Sarah spent time with Amy's parents, trying to be both honest about the possibilities but optimistic that this would be a case where the progression would halt and a swift recovery would follow. She watched as her patient and the parents set off towards the radiology department with the two consultant specialists in attendance. There was nothing more she could do for Amy now other than to keep her fingers crossed.

Sarah's attention to detail when checking the other two measles cases was even more than usually meticulous so it was mid-morning before she could look in on Alice Forster. The girl was still in her bed.

'She says she doesn't want to get up today.' Isobel Forster looked worried. A Walt Disney video was playing but Alice seemed uninterested.

'What's up, sweetheart?' Sarah let her hand rest on the small forehead briefly. 'Does something hurt?'

Alice shook her head a little. 'Not really.'

'I think we might take your temperature again.' Sarah smiled.

'It was normal this morning,' Isobel informed her.

Sarah was lifting the stethoscope from around her neck. 'I'm in super-doctor mode today. Let's just check everything. You don't mind, do you, darling?'

Rewarded by a now rare smile, Sarah put her earpieces in place and asked Alice to take a big breath.

'And again, sweetheart.'

This time Alice coughed as she exhaled and Sarah caught her expression.

'Does it hurt you to cough, Alice?'

'Just a bit.'

'Has she been coughing much?' Sarah directed the question at Isobel who shook her head.

'Maybe once or twice in the night.'

'OK.' Sarah clicked on a small torch. 'Let's have a look at that throat. Say Ah-h!'

On the face of it there didn't seem anything significantly different about Alice, but Sarah's instincts told her something was brewing. The temperature was raised but only fractionally, the cough was dry and there were no worrying sounds in her lungs, no redness in either her throat or ears. It was the child's dullness that bothered Sarah.

'Keep an eye on her and call me if you're worried,' she told Isobel. 'I'll ask Angela to increase her observations and I'll pop back when I can.'

As she was due to see Charlotte Newman for a

discharge examination Sarah poked her head only briefly into Michael's room.

'Hope you've been practising hard, Michael. I've got something special lined up for you today.'

Michael grinned and waved a crutch at her, narrowing missing Judith who was straightening his bed. She tried to look cross but didn't quite manage it.

Sarah spent the rest of the morning in Theatre, watching the repair of baby Jack's cleft lip and palate. The surgeon carefully marked points on the baby's face with a pen.

'Stand over here, Sarah. You'll get a better view. I'm putting these landmarks on to make sure we end up getting things as symmetrical as possible. It's easy to lose sight of where things need to go once we've opened everything up.'

He began to inject local anaesthetic into the baby's lips. 'This reduces the bleeding,' he explained to Sarah. 'It also builds up the tissues so they're easier to cut.'

Sarah watched in fascination throughout the two-and-a-half-hour operation and was admiring of the finished result. The surgeon stood back but shook his head.

'I can always find something I think I could have improved on.' He stripped off his gloves. 'He'll look a lot worse in a month's time. The scar tissue contracts and looks terrible but it eases off again. In three or four months we'll have a much better idea of the result.'

'It looks wonderful,' Sarah assured him. 'I'm really impressed.'

'I'm really hungry.' The surgeon grinned. 'That was a long haul. How about some lunch?'

Sarah glanced at the clock on the wall. It was just after 1 p.m. 'I'd love to,' she said apologetically, 'but I can't. I've got a patient waiting.'

A hurried trip back to her car allowed Sarah to collect a large paper bag that was sitting on her passenger seat. Then she made her way to Ward 23.

A few minutes later, carrying the adult-sized crutches under one arm and the paper bag under the other, Sarah took Michael down in the lift, through the busy main foyer and out into the courtyard area between the main hospital wing and the administration wing. A few staff members were enjoying some sunshine during their lunch break, dotted about the seating provided in the area. Sarah pointed to an unoccupied seat on one side of the courtyard area.

'That's your goal,' she told Michael.

'What?' Michael's eyes narrowed suspiciously.

'And that's mine.' Sarah indicated another bench seat on the other side of the paved area. It happened to be the seat on which she had sat with Paul Henderson the night she'd been on call and had found out about what he'd called his 'previous life'. Well, that little episode now belonged to her own 'previous life', Sarah thought bitterly. Past history. Brief and best forgotten. She turned over the paper bag and tipped out the light plastic soccer ball it contained. Michael's jaw dropped. He began to turn away.

'Wait a sec,' Sarah ordered. She adjusted her crutches, standing on one leg, then balanced on one crutch and swung the other carefully to contact the light ball. It skated over the paving and she hopped after it.

'Ready?' she called. Turning, Sarah hit the ball back towards Michael. It rolled to a stop in front of him. With an expression of having to humour an idiot, Michael shifted his balance, lifted his crutch and tapped the ball without enthusiasm. It rolled only a few inches.

'Come on, Michael,' Sarah shouted. 'Boot it!'

Michael hopped forward a step, settled his balance and took a healthier swipe at the ball. It flew up in the air, bounced and rolled well past Sarah.

'Yes!' she yelled. She turned and hopped after it but suddenly Michael was there as well. He must have put in a lot of practice over the weekend because his speed and balance had improved enormously. Sarah tried to hit the ball but Michael's crutch made first contact. He kept it under control, dribbling it along in front of him until he reached the bench.

'Goal,' he shouted. 'I win!'

'Hang on a minute,' Sarah protested. 'What happened to half-time?'

They spent a happy ten minutes, playing, until Sarah could see Michael was tiring. She put the ball under her own bench for the first time and then sat down on it.

'OK, you win. Three goals to one.'

Michael hopped over, the signs of tiredness gone.

'I thought you were tired,' Sarah said.

Michael grinned. 'I thought you needed a goal.' He sat down beside Sarah.

'Cheat!' Sarah told him affectionately. She put her arm around the boy's shoulders. 'You can go home tomorrow, Michael. I'll miss you.'

Michael glanced up shyly. 'I'll miss you, too.'

'You can keep the ball,' Sarah told him. 'When you get used to your new leg give me a ring and we'll have another game.'

Michael looked dubious and then a familiar sullen expression began to appear. Sarah gave him a feather-light punch on his arm.

'Hey! You've gone from not walking to playing soccer in the space of a few days. Your attitude is the only thing that could hold you back from now on, Michael. I know you can do anything you want. You know that too, don't you?' Sarah leaned down to look sternly at the boy beside her. 'Don't you?' she repeated.

'I guess.'

'Yeah, I guess too.' Sarah smiled. 'And I guess I better get back to work.' She stood up, extending a hand to Michael. As she straightened her gaze swept up the administration block. Right up to the fourth floor. Framed against the window of his office stood Paul Henderson. She was too far away to read his expression but it was clearly him and he had obviously been watching her. For how long? Sarah wondered, cursing her body yet again for the painful signals it was sending. Taking a deep breath, she tore her gaze away from the window and shook back her hair.

'Come on, Michael,' she said firmly. 'It's time to go.'

*   *   *

Martin Lynch's firm was on take for Paediatrics the next day, meaning frequent trips for Sarah to the emergency department which had to be managed on top of her normal ward and outpatient duties. Her first case, a nasty dose of croup, was admitted for observation. While the baby's breathing sounds were marked and continuous and the pulse rate high there was no indication of significant airway obstruction. The parents were confident of the history of the illness so there was no question of an inhaled foreign body, smoke or chemicals involved. An allergic reaction was also unlikely.

The cause was most probably viral and could well resolve rapidly but Sarah wanted the insurance of having intensive care and intubation facilities available should the situation deteriorate. Even with this degree of difficulty in breathing, the illness was terrifying to both parents and child and Sarah dispensed reassurance in large doses.

She accompanied the family up to the ward and took the opportunity to look in on Alice. Her temperature had returned to normal and she seemed brighter but Isobel told Sarah she had been coughing more during the night. Still uneasy, Sarah checked her carefully again and left instructions for the increased observations to continue.

The busy day was exactly what she needed. Her anger at both Paul and herself had receded but had been replaced by an acute sense of disillusionment. It required quite an effort to remain outwardly as cheerful and optimistic as normal but Sarah was confident she was managing. Saying goodbye to Michael nudged her spirits down further and she was glad of the call to Emergency that came shortly after.

'A two-year-old boy, Jamie Wilson,' the registrar informed Sarah. 'He collapsed while walking with his mother a short time ago. Apparently only unconscious for a few seconds and no seizure activity noted. He'd appeared normal since but she brought him in because she's worried. Heart rate is 52 beats a minutes and irregular. Blood pressure is 98 over 60 and the respiration rate is twenty a minute.' He showed her the ECG strip he was holding.

'It's an abnormally slow rate with complete heart block,' Sarah confirmed. 'There's the odd premature ventricular beat as well. Has he had any diagnosis made of congenital heart disease?'

'Not according to his mother.'

Sarah examined the child and they took another ECG trace. She questioned the mother carefully but could discover nothing very helpful. Jamie had been looked after by his grandmother earlier in the day. Sarah sent Mrs Wilson to ring her mother. 'Check whether he had any falls and knocked his head or chest. Or he may have eaten something odd. Get her to check the bathroom cabinet for any drugs in the house.'

Sarah ordered a chest X-ray and blood work-up, booked an echocardiogram and called in a cardiologist. The boy's heart rate was still far too slow and his level of consciousness was dropping. She also contacted the intensive care unit.

Mrs Wilson rushed back into the room at the same time as the cardiology registrar arrived.

'My mother went to check around the house—

that's why I took so long. She says the bottle of tablets on her bedside table is empty. She doesn't know how many there were—'

'What tablets were they?' Matt interrupted.

'They were for her heart—digoxin?'

Sarah and the cardiology registrar nodded. 'How long since he took them?' he asked.

'It's only an hour since I collected him but he was with her for about three hours. She doesn't know when he went into her room exactly but he did go looking for the cat about halfway through the visit.'

'We're too late for ipecac,' Sarah commented. She looked down at the little boy who was now unconscious. 'Is it still worth doing a gastric lavage?'

'Has he eaten anything since that time?'

Mrs Wilson shook her head. 'We were going home for tea—that's when he fainted.'

'It's worth doing,' the cardiology registrar told Sarah. 'We don't know how many tablets he took and he may still have quite a lot undigested.'

Matt Warnock nodded. 'Can I leave you to it, Sarah? We've got a serious MVA on the way in.'

Sarah was already busy with her preparations. 'Of course, Matt.' She turned to the nurse. 'Make sure it's a cuffed endotracheal tube,' she ordered.

'I'll get a lignocaine drip set up,' the cardiology registrar told her. 'And we'd better have an emergency pacemaker tray ready. I don't want to see that heart rate drop much further. We'll need some more bloods, too. We'll have to monitor serum potassium and digoxin levels carefully.'

Sarah donned a plastic apron and gloves. Tilting the boy's head back, Sarah gently inserted the cuffed endotracheal tube to protect his airway. Then she quickly measured the distance between his chin and umbilicus, marking the distance on the orogastric tube before inserting it.

'I'll have the syringe, thanks.' Sarah aspirated the stomach contents carefully with the syringe and then connected rubber tubing and a funnel to the orogastric tube.

'Have you warmed the saline?'

The nurse nodded. Sarah watched as she cut the bag and poured the saline into the funnel Sarah was holding.

'Whoa! That's enough.' Sarah lowered the funnel. 'Put that basin a bit further over here.' Splashed with the liquid now able to empty through the tubing, Sarah was glad of the large apron. She repeated the cycle several more times, before removing the tubing.

The IV line was in place, blood samples taken and drip started by the time Sarah had removed her apron and gloves.

'I'll get him up to ICU,' the cardiology registrar told her. 'They're ready for us. They've got the digoxin specific antibodies in already. Hopefully we'll get him back to you before too long.'

The emergency department was chaotic with the arrival of victims from a multiple MVA as Sarah left. She decided to walk the long way around the outside of the building to get back to the ward. A few minutes' peace and quiet and some fresh air were just what she needed.

Following the river-bank, which led to the car park behind the administration block, Sarah paused for a moment to watch the ducks and think about Alice. When a tiny movement in the grass caught her eye she ignored it initially. Then she looked again.

'I don't believe it!' she whispered aloud. Dropping to a crouch, Sarah peered into the grass. The movement of the blades progressed and Sarah leaned forward onto her knees.

The voice came from behind her. 'Sarah, what on earth are you doing? Are you all right?'

'Shh!' Sarah commanded. She watched intently, still on her knees. When she saw the renewed quivering in the grass ahead of her she cupped both hands and lunged carefully.

'Yes!'

'What in God's name are you up to, Sarah Kendall?' Paul demanded.

Sarah stood up slowly, her cupped hands held against her chest. Her eyes shining, she slowly lifted her thumbs.

Paul stepped closer. His head almost brushed hers as he looked down. Nestled into the cup of Sarah's palms was a tiny duckling—a ball of yellow and black fluff, with bright black eyes and a miniature beak that now opened to emit a series of worried peeps.

'I don't believe it,' Paul whispered. 'It's completely the wrong time of year for ducklings.'

'I don't believe it either,' Sarah said softly.

Paul looked around, scouting the grass and

nearby river. 'I can't see any more. And there's no sign of the mother. It's weird.'

'It's a miracle,' Sarah breathed.

'What on earth are you going to do with it? It won't survive if you let it go.'

'I've got no intention of letting it go,' Sarah said calmly. She looked at Paul for the first time. 'It's Alice Forster's greatest wish to see a duckling before she dies. We didn't think there was any hope of it happening at this time of year. I even rang all the farms where I knew people to see if I could get hold of one.' Sarah had to blink back the sudden moisture in her eyes. 'And now she's not only going to see one but she can touch it—keep it with her in her room.' Sarah bent her head and a tear she couldn't block dropped onto the duckling's head.

Paul extended a finger and gently swept the drop of moisture from the soft fluff. Then he cupped his hands over Sarah's and enclosed the duckling again.

'You're the most amazing person I've ever met, Sarah Kendall.'

The words and tone caressed her, and when Sarah met his eyes she felt the huge weight she had been carrying for the last few days begin to melt away. But his next words halted the process.

'I'm just sorry you have such a low opinion of me.'

Sarah stiffened. 'What did you expect, Paul? That I would be happy to share you?'

'No. I wasn't sure.' Paul sighed. 'As you said yourself, things happened too fast and they were

too big. I wanted just a little more time. I know
having a dependent child is enough to put some
women off. I've been there before.'

'Not to mention a dependent wife,' Sarah
snapped. 'Or was that going to wait just a little
longer as well?'

'No, I wasn't going to mention her,' Paul said
quietly. 'And it's an ex-wife, despite your obvious
assumptions. Catherine walked out on me when
Daniel was fourteen months old. We haven't seen
her since. And I haven't wanted to. She's past history and I'd prefer her to stay that way. The birth
of my son was the only good thing to come from
what was obviously a huge mistake—an error of
judgment that I was hardly likely to want to discuss
with a woman I had just fallen in love with.'

Sarah's eyes widened. *Had.* He had used the past
tense. Even his tone suggested that it was just another part of his 'past history'. She felt a sharp pain
knife through her body. 'I—I'm sorry, Paul. I didn't
think—'

'No. You didn't.' Paul looked away. He slid his
hands into his pockets. 'What you did think was
that I could lie about my feelings simply to entice
a partner for an extramarital affair. I find that in-
sulting. And very disappointing. You didn't trust
me.'

Sarah swallowed hard. He was right and she
couldn't think of a thing to say in her own defence.
The silence that fell was an abyss which Sarah felt
in danger of falling into.

'Paul?' Sarah queried in a small voice.

'Yes?' The blue eyes were carefully blank, as though a shield had been erected.

'Could I—could I borrow your handkerchief, please? This duckling's done something a bit yucky in my hand.'

Paul closed his eyes briefly and then his lips twitched. He pulled the white silk triangle that decorated the top pocket of his jacket and shook it out. Silently he handed it to Sarah.

'Thank you.' Sarah gently transferred the duckling into the handkerchief and then carefully tucked it into her white coat pocket. She bent to wipe her hand on the grass. When she looked up Paul was gone. She straightened, watching his back as he strode towards the car park with his hands back in his pockets.

Was it just the excitement that explained the flushed cheeks and sparkling eyes? Sarah watched as Alice reverently touched the duckling, sitting on her bed.

'Is he mine, Sarah?'

'He's all yours, darling.'

'Can I keep him?' The joy in the child's voice brought a huge lump to Sarah's throat. She was aware that Isobel was crying silently.

'Of course you can, sweetheart. For as long as you want.' Sarah sat on the edge of the bed. 'My mum knows all about raising ducklings and she'll tell me what we need to feed him. When he's too big to live in your bed he can go on her duck pond.'

'He'll never be too big,' Alice whispered breathlessly. 'He can swim in that big washing bowl we use for my bath.' She stopped suddenly, coughing.

Sarah frowned and reached for her stethoscope. 'Let me have a listen to your back, Alice.' She helped her sit forward and pulled up her pyjama jacket gently. 'You decide on a name for that little fluffball while I check you out.'

A few minutes later Sarah caught Isobel's eye. 'Her temperature's up and I can hear a few crackles. We'll start some antibiotics, I think.'

Isobel's eyes flashed with alarm. 'Bronchitis?' she queried quietly.

'Could be.' Sarah folded her stethoscope. Her instincts told her it was more likely to be pneumonia but she didn't want to put her fear into words. Both women knew what that would mean.

'I know what I'm going to call him.'

'What's that, darling?' Sarah returned Alice's happy smile.

'Ping.'

Following her mother's instructions, Sarah arrived at the hospital the next morning armed with tinned cat food, wholemeal bread and a pair of tweezers. She had to walk through a line of picketing cleaners to get to the main entrance and the obvious escalation of the problem made her think of Paul. She had taken the crumpled and stained handkerchief home to wash. She knew she could use it as an excuse to see Paul again, but would he even want to see her?

The confused jumble of her thoughts had led to a sleepless night. She blamed herself and then became angry at Paul again. Why should he have expected such complete trust so instantly? Wasn't that pure arrogance on his part? She didn't even know him.

But you reciprocated, she told herself. You agreed that you didn't need the 'entrée'. You matched his passion physically. If she hadn't been prepared to trust him how could she have done that? It put the encounter on a purely physical level, which disgusted her. OK, she admitted, she had trusted him—or had wanted to trust him. But who wouldn't have made the same assumption she'd made when confronted by his son? Was that so hard for him to understand?

Sarah wanted desperately to put things right, but Paul had walked away from her. Would her pride allow her to crawl back and beg for forgiveness? At the moment the answer was no, but the white silk handkerchief could wait. A symbol of potential resolution. A flag of surrender maybe, Sarah thought with a crooked grin.

Ping ate his breakfast enthusiastically and Sarah made herself late for her paediatric outpatient clinic, by staying to watch the duckling's first swim in the large enamel basin. Isobel followed her out as she left.

'She's worse, isn't she, Sarah?'

Sarah nodded. The chest X-ray had confirmed her fears that pneumonia was setting in. 'We're doing all we can, Isobel. You know that, don't you?'

Isobel nodded. Her voice caught. 'I've never seen her this happy, though. You, finding that duckling. It was…it's…'

'Magic,' Sarah said firmly. 'That's what it is.' She gave Isobel a quick hug. 'Enjoy it as much as

you can—both of you—and call me if you need
me.'

The call came even before the clinic was finished. Sarah called Martin Lynch in as well. He
examined Alice gently. The child was feverish and
very drowsy. The consultant's look as he finished
his examination told Sarah all she needed to know.
Isobel had also caught his expression and she
turned away suddenly towards the window, wrapping her arms tightly around herself.

Sarah placed an arm around her shoulders. 'I'll
come back as soon as I can. We'll see this through
together.'

The calls to other patients were an unwelcome
distraction through that long afternoon. When she
was called to the intensive care unit she found
Jamie Wilson's potassium and digoxin levels were
falling and he was back in a normal heart rhythm
and rate. Sarah made the necessary arrangements to
have him transferred to the ward. He would need
continued monitoring and treatment for at least a
week until his digoxin levels were under the toxic
range.

Normally she would have been thrilled with the
rapid recovery her other young transfer to the unit
had made. Amy Turner was out of danger and also
ready to move back to the ward, but even the
delight of all the parents involved failed to lift
Sarah's spirits. Her responses were automatic, the
focus of her thoughts too narrow to allow emotional
involvement with these cases. It was a relief when
her shift ended and there were no more calls to
interrupt the vigil she was sharing with Isobel.

Alice's level of consciousness slipped further, and as darkness fell her breathing became quieter. Dangerously quiet. Still she held on and at one point roused enough to ask for Ping. Isobel lifted the duckling from the small box he was in beside her pillow and cupped Alice's hand around him. It was a struggle for her to keep her eyes open but she managed a smile.

'I love you, Mummy.'

'And I love you, darling.' Isobel's cheek was laid gently against her daughter's, the tiny body cradled in her arms. Sarah perched on the side of the bed, one hand stroking Alice's head gently, the other on Isobel's shoulder.

It seemed an eternity and yet it seemed no time at all until Alice's laboured attempts to breathe finally ceased. Still they remained there, the three of them, physically connected, though now only two suffered any pain.

The pain was unbearable. Sarah finally left Isobel to have some time alone with her daughter for the last time. Unseeing, she stumbled outside and collapsed on a bench in the courtyard. The familiarity of that particular bench didn't even register. She buried her face in her hands and her whole body shook uncontrollably but silently. No tears would come—the pain was too intense.

Sarah was unaware that anybody had come until she felt arms, drawing her close. She had no need to uncover her face to know to whom they belonged. She felt the warmth and comfort available and buried her face against the hard chest.

'Alice just died,' she whispered brokenly.

Then the tears came, racking sobs that would have embarrassed her if she'd been aware of making them. Eventually the soothing words and stroking movements of the hands that held her permeated her misery. She struggled to control herself and gratefully accepted the handkerchief Paul produced.

'That's two you owe me,' he told her seriously.

Sarah laughed through her tears and Paul drew her against his chest again.

'I intend to collect the debt.' He stroked Sarah's hair back where the strands had caught on her damp face. 'I'm sorry, Sarah. I'm sorry that Alice has died and I'm sorry I gave you a hard time.' He brushed a tear from her cheek with his thumb. 'I expected too much too soon. I know that.' Bending his head, he placed his lips against her hair. 'It was only because I wanted to give you that much myself. Can you understand that?'

Sarah blew her nose inelegantly and then nodded.

'And can you trust me?'

Sarah raised her eyes and met the plea in Paul's. 'Yes,' she breathed. 'I'm sorry, too, Paul. I knew I could trust you. I just wouldn't let myself believe it.'

'Well, now you can,' Paul said firmly. 'Now I'm taking you home—and I'm staying. You can't be alone tonight.'

'But what about Daniel?'

'Our housekeeper lives in the same apartment block. She knew I might be late tonight with this meeting with the cleaners' union. She'll be happy to stay overnight. I'll just need to get back in time to see Daniel for breakfast and take him to school. Is that all right with you?'

'Oh, yes.' Sarah sighed. 'Yes, please.'

CHAPTER FIVE

'This is a first for me,' Sarah whispered. She held tightly to the hand of her companion.

'I hope it's the last,' Paul said solemnly.

'I'm not sure I can cope.' Sarah took a deep breath. 'What if I break down and make a spectacle of myself?'

'Nobody can make a spectacle of themselves, crying at a child's funeral,' Paul told her softly. He squeezed her hand. 'Amazingly enough, I've still got plenty of hankies.'

Sarah smiled guiltily. She still hadn't returned the two he'd already loaned her.

They sat quietly, holding hands and waiting as the tiny old chapel in the grounds of the hospital filled to overflowing with Alice's friends, her mother's family and the many staff who had been touched by Alice Forster's short life. Alice's father was noticeable only by his absence, much to Sarah's relief.

The service was simple—and very moving. Sarah cried openly as did everybody there, including the minister. When Sarah looked up to see the tears on Paul's cheek she used the crumpled, borrowed handkerchief to wipe them away. Their eyes met and the sadness they shared added yet another link in the chain that was binding them together. Still holding hands, they later walked beside the river.

'What happened to the duckling?' Paul queried.

'I took him out to my parents,' Sarah replied. 'He's doing fine. Mum's got a real knack with young creatures. He can go and live on their duck pond when he's older.' She sighed and then smiled wistfully. 'I guess a little bit of the magic did rub off on Alice after all.'

'What's that?'

Sarah just smiled again. 'Thanks for coming today, Paul.'

'She touched my life, too, you know.' Paul drew Sarah into his arms. 'Do you realise it was Alice who was responsible for us meeting?'

Sarah nodded and then lifted her head up. Paul kissed her softly.

'Would you come and have dinner with me tonight?' he asked.

'What about Daniel?'

'I meant with us. At our apartment.'

Sarah hesitated. 'I don't think Daniel's too keen on me. He wouldn't even say anything the morning I met him.'

Paul sighed heavily. 'Daniel's very wary of women. Any that he's cared about have abandoned him. First his mother and then a nanny he got very attached to. He keeps his distance now.' Paul kissed Sarah again. 'But it's only a matter of time. He's very like me and I know he'll love you when he gets to know you. How could he help it?'

Sarah basked in the warmth of the look she received but then her brow creased.

'I think it might be a bit threatening to invade

his home just yet. Why don't we meet on neutral territory?'

Paul nodded. 'I forgot you majored in child psychology. What do you suggest?'

'Something fun. Why don't we go out to Orana Park on Saturday? I'll borrow my niece and dilute the atmosphere a bit more.'

Paul grinned. 'Great. God, I hope you'll like him.'

'If he's just like you, how could I help it?'

The pain of losing Alice had affected Sarah's work that week. The flow of admissions, outpatients and emergencies kept up but Sarah found it quite easy to keep a professional distance. One nine-year-old boy who bravely battled through a severe asthma attack nearly broke through the self-erected barrier but the room to which he was admitted had been that of Alice Forster. Now stripped bare of the personal furnishings and decorations, it felt to Sarah as though the room had also died. She kept her visits to a professional minimum. She would be glad when this run ended in a couple of weeks. It was time for a break and maybe a complete change.

Alice Forster seemed to have been quite symbolic, Sarah mused. She had been admitted for the first time during Sarah's first week on the ward and now this chapter in her life felt like it was coming to a close. Alice had also been the catalyst for something Sarah now knew would form the next chapter.

The impression of the child's importance in her life was heightened on Friday afternoon when Sarah found Isobel Forster, waiting to see her. The two women embraced fondly and then Sarah stepped back to search her friend's face.

'How are you, Isobel? I've been thinking about you all the time.'

'I'm taking things one day at a time,' Isobel responded. 'I'm OK, I guess.'

'The service was very special.' Sarah smiled. 'She was a much-loved little girl.'

Isobel nodded. 'How's Ping?'

'Doing very well. Growing fast by all accounts.'

'I'll never forget you, doing that for Alice,' Isobel said quietly. 'It made the end the happiest time she had in here. I really just wanted to thank you—but words are so inadequate.'

Sarah smiled gently. 'You don't need to thank me. I loved Alice too. I'll never forget her.'

'There's something I want you to have.' Isobel fished in her shoulder-bag. She drew out the yellow velvet duck and pressed it into Sarah's hands. 'Keep it,' she begged. 'I hope one day you have a little girl of your own. Maybe the duck will remind you of Alice sometimes and the memory will make you treasure your own child even more.'

Sarah was still holding the soft yellow duck when she left the ward for the day an hour later. She wondered again at the amazing bond she had witnessed so often between mothers and their children. Sometimes it had evoked a feeling akin to jealousy in her. Would she ever be able to give and receive the kind of unconditional love the bond represented?

At present, her future contained the possibility of

a stepchild. While she knew that bond could never be quite the same, it could still be very rewarding. But what if Daniel refused to accept her in his life? Would that be enough to destroy what she and Paul had found in each other? Sarah felt very nervous about their planned excursion the next day.

Her nervousness increased when they met at the entrance to the safari park on Saturday afternoon. Daniel refused to make eye contact when introduced and he ignored Holly's greeting. Holly rolled her eyes at Sarah. They all remained silent as they purchased their tickets.

'Where to first?' Paul studied the map he held. 'We've got thirty minutes until the lion feeding. Shall we take a guided tour or go walking?'

'What would you like to see, Daniel?' Sarah made an effort to sound casual.

'Dunno.' The tone was sullen and Holly made another face at Sarah.

'I want a ride on the train,' Holly announced. 'We'll have to be quick—it's about to go.'

'Come on, then.' Paul set off and they all followed, climbing on board the trailer being pulled by a tractor. Paul sat down first and Sarah moved to sit beside him but somehow Daniel got there first. He made eye contact with Sarah then and his look was triumphant. Sarah repressed a smile at the unsubtle hint and sat behind them with Holly at her side. Separated, and with the commentary of the guide making conversation impossible, Sarah tried to relax. She had hoped that the two children might hit it off and make things easier but so far the outgoing Holly was clearly unimpressed by Daniel's reserve.

Things got worse at the lion feeding. Daniel refused to handle the lumps of raw meat they were offered. Holly took two, threw them down the tube and peered after them to see the lions snatch and devour the food. Then, her fingers covered in blood, she raised her hands and wiggled her fingers in Daniel's face.

'Beware the ghost of doom!' she intoned in a hollow voice.

'Get lost,' Daniel replied. He stepped back to stand close to Paul.

Sarah caught Paul's eye. He rolled his eyes in a good imitation of Holly's earlier reaction but he looked worried at the same time. She pointed Holly in the direction of a water trough. 'Wash off the ghost of doom,' she ordered. 'We'll go and see the tigers and then find some afternoon tea.'

They set off, the adults setting a brisk pace. Holly kept up with them but Daniel lagged behind a little, radiating disapproval.

'He's a bit of a nerd, isn't he?' Holly whispered loudly to Sarah.

'Shh! Give him a chance,' Sarah responded quietly. 'Why don't you try talking without us around?'

'OK.' Holly slackened her pace to allow Daniel to catch up.

'At least she's not shy,' Paul commented. Walking side by side, their hands brushed together as Paul moved closer to talk. Sarah resisted the impulse to hold hands. That certainly wouldn't improve the ambience of the outing.

'I'm sorry this is so difficult,' Paul apologised.

'I didn't expect it to be easy,' Sarah assured him. 'Don't worry. I don't give up that easily.'

The children were still behind them by several paces but Holly's voice carried clearly. 'She's not my mother—she's my aunt. I haven't got a father.'

'Well, I haven't got a mother.' Sarah listened keenly as she heard Daniel begin to talk for the first time. 'I don't want one either.'

Sarah tried to catch Paul's eye but he'd closed them, his expression a silent groan.

'Well, I don't want a father,' Holly announced. 'So there! My mum says they're surflous.'

'Superfluous.' Sarah couldn't help providing the correction.

'What's that?' Daniel's query was a suspicious growl.

'Um. More than what you really need.'

'See?' Holly's tone was triumphant. 'Sarah thinks so too.'

'Hey, wait on! I never said that!' Sarah looked over her shoulder to frown at her niece but Holly's cheeky grin warned her that the conversation wasn't finished.

'Your dad is Sarah's boyfriend,' Holly informed Daniel.

'He is not!'

'Course he is, stupid. Why do you think they're going out together?' She lowered her voice. 'They'll probably get married.'

Paul's stifled groan carried only to Sarah's ears. She didn't dare look at him.

'They will not.' Daniel was ready for a fight. 'My dad's never going to get married again. He says there's two of us to get married to and he doesn't believe there's anybody that special in the whole world.'

Sarah was sure she could feel the heat of his glare directed at the back of her head. Holly, however, wasn't impressed.

'Well, my mum says she bets anything that this is *it*. She said if he's managed to hold her interest for more than five minutes he must be something amazing. And she said it's about time and something about a clock.'

'A clock?' Paul's despairing look had given way to frank amusement. He dropped back to wait for Holly. 'What did your mum say to you about a clock?'

'I'm not sure,' Holly confessed. 'She was talking to Gran, not me.'

'You shouldn't have been eavesdropping,' Sarah admonished. 'And you certainly shouldn't be repeating what you heard.'

'You told me to talk to him,' Holly told her aunt accusingly. 'It was the most interesting thing I could think of.'

'Can we go home now, Dad?' Daniel glared at his father.

'Soon.' Paul sighed. Then he flashed a grin at Sarah, before turning back to Holly. 'So, what did your gran say after that bit about the clock?'

'Paul!' Sarah was horrified, but they both ignored her.

'Gran said that anyone that puts that sort of sparkle in Sarah's eye is OK by her and she was going to keep her fingers crossed.'

'That was an unmitigated disaster!'

'Oh, I don't know. I really like Holly. Are you all so outspoken in your family?'

Sarah rested her head on Paul's shoulder. They had found a secluded bench on the river-bank and for once their lunch breaks had coincided.

'And I thought taking Holly might help,' Sarah said with a sigh. 'It couldn't have been worse, could it?'

'Nope.' Paul sounded remarkably cheerful. 'But you don't give up easily, remember?'

'I'll think of something,' Sarah promised. 'Hey, I'm not on call tonight. Any chance of you getting away?'

'I'll talk to Mrs Henry.'

'Is she your housekeeper?'

'Yes. She's a widow and seems glad of the extra cash. Daniel doesn't like it but he's having to get used to it, what with all the out-of-hours meetings the cleaners' dispute has caused.'

'Was Daniel the real reason you went into management?'

Paul nodded. 'I found I didn't really know my son. There he was, about to start school, and his upbringing had been left to a series of live-in nannies and housekeepers. His behaviour was deteriorating and I suddenly realised I had a very lonely and unhappy little boy on my hands. I had to change something pretty drastically and the long hours at work and on call seemed an obvious place to start. I did think I could do a good job in management but it was the hardest thing I've ever done—leaving surgery.'

'Has it helped Daniel?'

'Oh, yes. We're much closer. He's still not as happy as I'd like him to be, though.'

'And neither are you.'

'I'm much happier than I was a couple of weeks ago.' Paul bent to plant a series of kisses on Sarah's face and lips. 'God, I'll make sure Mrs Henry is available tonight. I'm having severe withdrawal symptoms.'

'Good.' Sarah scrambled to her feet after a quick glance at her watch. 'I'd hate to think I was suffering alone.'

As they walked back to the main entrance together Sarah suddenly chuckled.

'What's so funny?'

'That I got so angry, thinking you were having an affair with me. It *is* like having an affair—snatching bits of time together. Only it's not your wife we have to worry about. It's your son.'

'I'm sorry things are complicated,' Paul said slowly, 'but I can't apologise for having Daniel. Until I met you he was the only person in the world that I would have sacrificed everything for. Now he's just got to accept that I'm not prepared to sacrifice my relationship with you.'

'It'll work out,' Sarah promised. 'It has to. I just need to find a key, that's all.' She paused thought-

fully as their paths diverged. 'Does Daniel want to
be a policeman when he grows up?'

'Good grief, I don't think so. What on earth
makes you ask?'

'It's just that when I saw him that first time he
was...uh...looking at a picture in a magazine. A
police handler and his dog. It looked as though it
might be significant.'

Paul laughed. 'It was the dog, not the policeman.'
His smile vanished. 'Daniel has a passion for dogs.
He's begged for one for years but there's just no
way I can accommodate it. Not with our lifestyle.'

'That's great!' Sarah enthused.

'Sorry?' Paul was clearly bewildered.

'You've just given me the key, I think. Keep
Saturday free. I'll pick you both up as soon as I
finish my ward round.'

Sarah's excitement about her plan and the sheer joy
that last night's few hours together had given her
had to be shelved the next day as she faced a hectic
time on take. The firm's houseman had to cope with
most of the ward duties as Sarah found herself unable to get away from the emergency department.

Her first case was a very distressed six-year-old,
David Hill, having his first severe asthma attack.
He was unable to use the peak flow monitor, but
with the help of his mother and a nurse Sarah was
able to attach a blood-pressure cuff and measure the
major swing in blood pressure caused by massive
respiratory effort against constricted airways. The
airway obstruction was severe. She started the nebuliser treatment another staff member had pre-

pared while she had been making her brief examination.

'We'll use compressed oxygen, not air,' Sarah reminded the junior houseman. 'We'll get an IV line in and start steroids as soon as we've completed this nebuliser.' She looked again at her young patient with concern. 'If there's no real improvement then I'll do an arterial stab to check blood gases and we'll repeat the nebuliser.'

Leaving the other staff to supervise David, Sarah went to see a twelve-year-old girl, Bonnie, who was waiting next door. Her mother looked very relieved to see Sarah.

'Bonnie's had this terrible headache for two days,' she explained. 'She fainted yesterday and we went to the GP. He said to go home and give her some paracetamol, but it was no better this morning and the doctor said to bring her straight in here. He said it could possibly be meningitis.'

Sarah examined the girl carefully. She was certainly very sick and had a stiff neck but there were no other indications of meningitis.

'Bonnie's obviously very unwell,' she told the mother. 'I can't say for sure what's wrong but certainly with her symptoms the possibility of meningitis has to be considered. She has some of the symptoms, like a stiff neck, but her pain is unusual in that it's quite localised to one side. Other signs I might expect are not there but there's only one way to be sure and that's to do a lumbar puncture. Have you heard of that, Bonnie?'

The girl shook her head miserably. Sarah explained the procedure and then went back to check on David while the nursing staff set up. Not too happy with his progress, she ordered a trolley and preparations for inserting an IV line and doing an arterial puncture. She smiled grimly at the emergency department registrar, Matt, who stopped her as she was heading back to Bonnie.

'We've got a very sick baby just come in. Severe gastroenteritis and looks pretty dehydrated.'

'I've got a lumbar puncture to do now.' Sarah frowned. 'Can you get an IV in and do an arterial stab on David Hill for me? I'll get to the baby in five minutes. What cubicle?'

'Four.' The registrar vanished behind David's curtain.

Sarah had Bonnie sitting up and leaning forward to perform the lumbar puncture. The procedure was over quickly and Sarah then inserted an IV cannula and arranged for the girl's admission.

'We'll know the results within a few hours,' she told them. 'In the meantime, we'll start some antibiotics and get you comfortable up in the ward, Bonnie.'

The baby was another girl, Paige, and she was also very ill. Fourteen months old, she had had vomiting and diarrhoea for several days, was running a high fever and looked terrible. Her eyes were quite sunken, her skin had lost much of its elasticity and felt cold and clammy. Her level of consciousness was still good, however, and she hadn't suffered any convulsions.

'We're going to need to replace the fluids Paige has lost,' Sarah explained to the distraught young parents. 'We'll have to admit her and keep a close eye on her for a day or two.'

Sarah weighed the baby and found she was nine kilograms. She smiled at the parents. 'That makes my job easier. I won't need a calculator.'

'Why's that?' Paige's father relaxed visibly at Sarah's smile.

'With the condition Paige is in we assume that she's lost eight to ten per cent of body weight so that is the amount we need to replace.' Sarah put on gloves and swabbed the baby's scalp. 'I'm going to put a tiny tube into a vein here so we can put the fluids through it.'

Paige's wails as the nurse restrained her made Sarah's job easier, distending the veins on her scalp, but it made it much more distressing for the mother. Sarah smiled sympathetically and then turned her attention to slipping the needle into the vein.

'It's twice as hard to have things done to your children as it is to have it done to yourself, isn't it? There, that's got it.' Sarah reached for a syringe and clipped it onto the end of the needle. 'I'm going to take a blood sample first and then we'll tape it down and attach the infusion.' She gave the baby back to her mother and nodded at the nurse.

'Make up 800 mils half-strength isotonic saline.' Sarah turned back to Paige's parents. 'We're going to admit Paige now and I'll be watching her very carefully for the next few hours. When we've replaced the fluids she's lost then we'll start another infusion at a slower rate to maintain her levels.'

Even when she finally made it up to the ward, having missed the lunchtime Paediatric meeting and presentation, Sarah found her time taken up completely by her new admissions.

David was improving slowly, but he still needed continuous nebuliser treatment as well as IV medication. Bonnie's mother was much happier, having professional help to care for her sick daughter, but Paige was concerning Sarah. Her electrolyte deficits meant frequent adjustments to the rate and strength of her infusion, and Sarah didn't feel confident that things were under control until she finally left the hospital at ten p.m.

In contrast, the atmosphere in the ward on Saturday morning was controlled and positive, and Sarah found all her new admissions improved. David was down to a nebuliser treatment at three- to four-hourly intervals, Paige was ready to be offered an oral feed and Bonnie's test results had ruled out meningitis. It now seemed likely that she was suffering from mycoplasma pneumonia, which would still mean observation for several days and a lengthy course of antibiotics. After a whirlwind catch-up on all her other patients Sarah was happy to leave the hospital.

The effects of the positive morning were still with her when she drove over to collect Paul and Daniel. She wasn't going to let the child's unresponsiveness undermine her optimism. Sarah refused to tell them where they were going until she turned into the long, tree-lined driveway of her parents' property. Having primed her mother, Sarah was pleased to see the whole family contingent of eight retrievers waiting to greet them. Her mother had even embellished the plan by coming out, hold-

ing a tiny representative of the latest litter. Sarah
saw Daniel smile for the first time when Evelyn
handed him the puppy.

'Look after this chap for me, Daniel. I'd better
get this mob under control.'

At the sharp whistle the dogs abandoned their
enthusiastic inspection of Paul and milled around
Evelyn. 'Sit!' she ordered.

Sarah saw the look of awe on Daniel's face as
all eight dogs sat and gazed adoringly at their mis-
tress. She was amused to find the expression mirrored exactly on Paul's face.

'Don't get out of line around here,' she warned
him. 'It's not worth it.'

'I've got every intention of behaving myself,'
Paul replied. He grinned at Sarah's father. 'How
come Sarah hasn't turned out to be the model of
obedience?'

'It's beyond me.' Jack laughed. 'Come and have
a beer before lunch.'

Evelyn and Daniel vanished into the puppies'
quarters. They still hadn't appeared thirty minutes
later after Paul had finished his first beer, admired
Ping's progress and had begun an animated conversation with Jack about the perspective a rural GP
had of the current health system. Sarah decided the
bacon and egg pie her mother had made was in dire
need of coming out of the oven. Evelyn and Daniel
appeared briefly at that point, wolfed down some
lunch and vanished again. Daniel shot a grin at his
father as he left.

'Evelyn's going to show me the obedience and

agility stuff she does. She says it's really easy to train a dog.'

Sarah felt a wrench at the child's grin and happy tone. God, he was so like his father. Paul gave her a thumbs-up sign. 'You were right,' he told her.

'What about?'

'Your mum's certainly got a knack with young creatures. I don't think I've ever seen him this happy.'

'This is the perfect place for kids.' Jack pushed his chair back. 'We don't get enough of them around here now. Plenty of dogs, though,' he added thoughtfully. 'And I guess there's not that much difference. Same need for constant feeding, same level of noise, same dirt being tracked through the house…'

Sarah laughed. 'At least we didn't shed hair!' She nudged Paul. 'Are you going to stop eating? I want to show you all my childhood haunts.'

It was getting dark by the time they drove back to the city. They stopped and had fish and chips for dinner at a country pub. Daniel didn't stop talking and the conversation was all about the dogs.

'It's quite hard to teach them scent-retrieving,' he explained to his father. 'What you do is carry around a hanky or something and make sure it's covered with your smell—'

Paul looked suspiciously at Sarah. 'Is *that* what you're doing with my hankies?'

If Daniel was disturbed by the look that passed between the adults he didn't show it. 'Then you have other hankies that don't have your scent on them. You have to use tongs or something to spread them around.'

Paul's and Sarah's gazes caught again and held. There was no need to speak. The wonderful afternoon they'd all had and the bubbly child now sitting with them was all the encouragement they could have hoped for.

'When the dog picks up the right one you have to praise it heaps. If it goes for the wrong one you just ignore it and put it back.'

Paul smiled at his son. 'Your dinner's getting cold, mate.'

Daniel looked embarrassed. 'I guess I'm talking too much. Sorry.'

'Don't be.' Sarah's lips curved into a gentle smile. 'I'm glad you had a good time, Daniel.'

'I did. Thanks.' Daniel looked away but then his eyes turned on his father. The pleading look in his eyes reminded Sarah of the retrievers they'd left behind. 'I wish I could have a dog, Dad.'

'Wishes come true occasionally,' Paul said thoughtfully. 'All you need is a bit of magic.'

'Yeah.' Daniel's face fell into familiar lines again. 'There's not much of that around, though, is there?'

'Oh, I don't know about that,' Sarah murmured. 'I've noticed a bit here and there.'

CHAPTER SIX

THE magic was about all right.

The sense of family they had achieved on Saturday was enough for both Paul and Sarah to feel confident that their own wish could come true. It was a week of frequent meetings, joyous love-making and excited plans.

'We'll get Daniel a dog!'

'Maybe two,' Sarah agreed.

'A house in the country!'

'Absolutely. How about a new job for you?'

'Terrific idea. But what about you?' Paul looked serious suddenly. 'I don't expect you to give up a promising career because of me and Daniel.'

'I'm not even sure what I want to do yet,' Sarah said. 'I'm seriously considering taking Martin Lynch up on his offer of part-time work in his private practice. I'd like the long- term follow-up that would give me on patients. General practice would be good for that as well. Dad will have to retire some time. And I'd have time to try other things. I'd like to write a book.'

'What sort of book?' Paul looked intrigued.

'Maybe a sort of practical paediatric guide for parents. What to worry about and what *not* to worry about. Maybe a bit of psychology thrown in as well.'

'You might need some first-hand experience,' Paul warned.

'I've got plenty of experience,' protested Sarah.

'Not as a parent,' Paul grinned wickedly. 'But that can be arranged. Come here.'

'No way! I'm not following in my sister's path. I intend to have a husband first.'

'That can also be arranged,' Paul promised. He kissed Sarah's neck, his hand lightly brushing her breast on a downward path.

'Mmm. Well, in that case...'

During her last week on her paediatric run Sarah seemed to be busier than ever. The joy she had found in her relationship with Paul spilled over into her professional life and nobody could fail to notice the change. Martin Lynch was delighted for his registrar.

'I knew he'd been impressed with you,' he said with a smile. 'I just didn't realise how much.'

Angela was astounded. She admired the huge diamond solitaire on Sarah's finger. 'I thought you said he was an unmitigated bureaucrat who didn't listen to anything you said.'

'I did say he was tall, dark and handsome as well.' Sarah twisted the ring on her finger.

Paul had dragged her away after her outpatient clinic the day before. They had trailed around numerous jewellery stores, with Sarah protesting all the way.

'We can't do this yet, Paul. Daniel's not ready.'

'We don't have to set a date,' Paul had argued.

'I just want some visible evidence that this is really happening. That you feel the same way I do.'

Sarah had met his intense gaze and had smiled gently. Then her smile had stretched to a grin. 'You haven't proposed yet.'

'Haven't I?' Paul looked horrified. To the amusement of the jewellery store manager, two assistants and several other customers, he dropped to one knee in front of the counter.

'Sarah Kendall, will you do me the honour of becoming my wife? I love you,' he added hastily.

Sarah's gurgle of laughter had the whole shop smiling. 'Of course I will. Please get up off the floor.'

The onlookers clapped as Paul scrambled to his feet. 'Right. Let's get on with finding this ring.'

The presence of the ring on her finger was a constant, though unnecessary, reminder to Sarah of how happy she felt. She was enjoying her ward round. Bonnie was finally ready for discharge and a much happier girl than when she'd been admitted with suspected meningitis the previous week.

'You'll need to stay on the antibiotics for another two weeks,' Sarah told her, 'but your chest sounds great and the X-ray we did this morning looks fine. We'll see you in the outpatient clinic when you've finished the course of pills.'

Not that she would be seeing her, Sarah realised with a pang. She wouldn't have any contact with these patients again and she still hadn't made any arrangements about what she was going to do. She touched the diamond on her finger as though it were a talisman. The future might be unknown but it would be shared, and that was enough to dispel any qualms.

Her visit to David Hill was also a happy one, despite the upper respiratory tract infection which had complicated the control of his asthma and delayed his recovery.

'You haven't had any dip in your morning peak flow rate for three days,' she congratulated him. 'We can take out the IV line now. We'll go back to your normal inhaler treatment and a course of pills. We'll keep you in for another day or two but then you can go home. Oh, look at this.' Sarah fished in her pocket. 'What do you think of this new inhaler holder?'

'Cool!' David's eyes lit up.

Sarah handed over the bright yellow plastic container in the shape of Bart Simpson's head. 'You can get a glow-in-the-dark Casper or Spiderman as well,' Sarah told him. 'And they're going to bring out Tweety Bird and Daffy Duck shortly.'

David looked at the sweatshirt Sarah was wearing again. 'I like Bart Simpson. Thanks, Dr Sarah.'

Sarah refused to be dismayed when she saw Angela's grim expression on her return to the office, but the nurses's words curtailed her optimism.

'We've got a re-admission coming in.'

'It's not Michael, is it?' The last report Sarah had had from the physiotherapist was that Michael was doing well—the fitting and adjustment of the artificial leg was progressing rapidly.

'No, not Michael. Worse.'

'Let me guess. Anthony?'

Angela nodded. 'His GP's referred him back. Another dose of pneumonia.'

'Probably the same one,' Sarah growled. 'I wonder just how successful his mother was at keeping up his medication.'

'IV treatment again, I suppose,' Angela said with a sigh.

'And for longer this time, I expect.' Sarah nodded. 'Call me when he gets here. We'll have to check for any underlying immunological problems as well.' She grinned ruefully. 'Lots of blood tests. Oh, excuse me, I want a word with Cheryl.'

She caught up with the physio. 'How's Michael?'

'Great,' Cheryl responded. 'He's coming in for an appointment this afternoon in the department. Why don't you come and see him?'

Sarah found them in the gymnasium later that day. Michael was walking between two bars, but only holding one. Wearing jeans and track shoes he looked like any other ten-year-old boy.

'Wow!' Sarah exclaimed. 'Which leg was it again?'

Michael's grin told her that was exactly what he wanted to hear. 'Watch this, Sarah!' Michael let go of the bar and walked unaided. His gait was a little stiff but his balance looked good.

'Where's the soccer ball?' Sarah smiled.

'I need a bit more practice first,' Michael admitted, 'but the kids at school are going to let me play when I'm ready.'

Sarah hugged him hard. 'I'm really proud of you, Michael. I'll bet you're proud of yourself, too.'

His grin was shy. 'Yeah, I guess.'

Anthony's re-admission was not quite as traumatic as Angela had feared. The little boy was sick enough not to put up too much of a physical struggle as Sarah took the blood tests and inserted an IV cannula. His hand looked like Fort Knox by the time she'd finished. The needle was covered with an upturned plastic container attached to the splint and stuck down with strong tape before the bandaging began.

'He'll never get that out,' she declared confidently. She watched the X-ray technician leave and wondered if she looked that harassed herself. While the physical struggle had been manageable the noise level had been exhausting. Sarah was very glad to escape herself.

It was unfortunate that Sarah decided to clear her in-basket at that point. Instead of recovering from her encounter with Anthony, she experienced a real slump in her mood. The blood tests were back on a little girl she had seen in her outpatient clinic the day before.

Two-year-old Natasha had been referred because of an apparent susceptibility to infection. While the illnesses had been minor their frequency had been causing concern and there was a suspicion of anaemia. Sarah's misgivings had been aroused on hearing that the child had suffered a nose-bleed recently, and her suspicions were now confirmed. Natasha was suffering from acute lymphoblastic leukaemia. Another Alice Forster, Sarah thought miserably. I couldn't go through that again. Ever.

Paul noticed her quietness when he met her after work. Sarah explained.

'She may do very well,' he encouraged her. 'The majority do these days.'

'There's still the trauma of the tests and treatments, though,' Sarah replied. 'And the agonising worry hanging over her parents for years.'

'It's the worst part of being a parent,' Paul agreed. 'Even when your child is perfectly healthy, like Daniel, there's always that fear that something might happen.'

They walked in silence to the car park.

'It doesn't happen very often, though. Your perspective gets skewed in a job like yours.'

Sarah nodded. 'It's time I took a break.'

'Do you feel up to tonight?'

She nodded again. 'I'll have to be back here by ten. I've agreed to cover for the neonatal unit. They still haven't filled their registrar position. They're putting a bit of pressure on me to give it serious consideration.' Sarah sighed. 'I hope I get some sleep but right now I'm more worried about this dinner tonight. Do you really think it's a good idea to tell Daniel yet?'

Paul waved as Sarah got into her car. 'I don't want to wait. I think he'll be thrilled when we tell him about our plans. Especially if he gets to have a dog.'

'I don't want a bloody dog!'

Daniel's language was no shock to Sarah but the anguished expression on his face certainly was. He looked from his father to Sarah and back again. The food on the table was ignored.

'You said we didn't need anybody else,' he accused Paul. 'You said we were a team.' His voice held the hint of tears.

'We *are* a team, Daniel,' Paul assured him gently. 'A great team. But Sarah could be part of the team.'

'Why?' Daniel struggled harder against the tears. 'Why do you want her?'

'I love Sarah, Daniel,' Paul said quietly.

'You said you loved me!' Sobs now punctuated the shouted words and Paul held out his arms to his son.

'I do love you, Daniel. More than anything.'

The small boy ignored the offered embrace. 'Not more than *her*!'

Silently Paul went to put his arms around his son but Daniel struggled free. He ran from the room and a door slammed loudly in the hall.

Paul started to move after him but stopped. 'I'll give him some time to calm down. Then we'll be able to talk.' He looked at Sarah who still sat at the table, staring down at her hands. 'I guess the house in the country wasn't enough.'

Sarah shook her head in agreement.

'Even the dog wasn't. I was sure that would swing it.'

Sarah looked up finally. 'This isn't going to work, Paul.'

Paul frowned. 'I thought you didn't give up easily.'

'This is different.'

'Why?' The tone was demanding. Sarah could see that the stress caused by Daniel's response to the news of their engagement had upset Paul

deeply. This wasn't the best time to discuss anything.

'Why?' Paul repeated, the word almost a bark.

Sarah took a deep breath. 'Daniel's bond with
you is the only security he's ever had. He's not
confident enough to share that.'

'Well, he'll have to learn.' Paul sounded angry
suddenly. 'It's something he'll just have to accept.'

'You can't force someone to accept something
emotional,' Sarah said quietly. 'It's not in your
power to control it.'

'He just needs some time.'

'No. It's too deeply rooted for that.' Sarah shook
her head.

'He doesn't have to accept it, then. But he'll have
to learn to live with it. I'm not giving you up,
Sarah.'

'It wouldn't work, Paul.' Sarah had been twisting
the ring on her finger. Now she eased it off. 'I'm
not going to jeopardise the relationship you have
with your son. You would only resent me for it.
Maybe not immediately but one day you would, and
it would be enough to undermine what we have
together and eventually to destroy it.' She placed
the ring carefully beside her plate and stood up.

Paul looked at the ring and then his gaze burned
into Sarah's eyes. 'So you're prepared to throw our
relationship away on the say-so of an eight-year-old
boy?'

'He's not just a boy, Paul. He's your son.' Sarah
picked up her bag. 'And I'd rather throw it away
than watch it being destroyed piece by piece.'

'This doesn't say much about the strength of the love you claim to have for me,' Paul said bitterly.

'Perhaps it says more than you think.' Sarah's voice was flat. The pain growing within her was too great to acknowledge.

'Well, if it's that easy for you to throw away, perhaps I don't want it. Why don't you just leave? Go on!' Paul turned his back and began to clear the table. The dishes clashed as he gathered them together angrily.

Sarah opened her mouth but no words came out. She wanted to run to Paul, to put her arms around him and erase the angry exchange. But the muffled sob she heard from behind the closed door in the hall made her pause. Paul walked into the kitchen and out of sight. The situation was impossible and any attempt to rectify it at this point would probably only make things worse. Sarah turned and stumbled from the apartment.

If only they had waited. They could have waited to tell Daniel about their engagement. More importantly, they could have waited to discuss his reaction to it. How could they possibly have been rational in the aftermath of the emotional scene and with the knowledge that a small boy was sobbing his heart out in the room next door? She shouldn't have been so quick with her negative prognosis either, Sarah thought miserably.

She parked her car behind the administration block of the hospital and rubbed her finger where the ring had been. Her natural optimism had declined with the stress of treating Anthony and had

hit bottom on learning of Natasha Ward's leukaemia. It hadn't had a chance to surface again, before
being faced with Daniel's anguish.

Why did it seem so easy for the sparks to ignite
between Paul and herself? For the anger to take
over and disguise the love so effectively? I suppose
it's the flip side of passion, Sarah admitted. Just like
the flip side of the joy of parenting is the worry
about a sick child. She headed towards her office
to collect her white coat and hoped she wouldn't
be faced with too many examples of that type of
anguish tonight.

The neonatal intensive care unit was almost full
that night but the situation was controlled and stable
when Sarah arrived. She was early and there were
no new admissions on the way so she sat at the
central desk, reviewing the notes. It was a distraction from her own misery and would allow her to
be prepared if any complications arose.

Sarah glanced up sharply as an apnoea alarm
sounded but the passing nurse merely flicked the
tiny baby's toes. The reminder to start breathing
again was effective and Sarah turned back to the
notes with a sigh. She needed more of a distraction
than this was providing. When her beeper sounded
she reached towards the phone with relief.

It was Paul. 'Sarah, I'm sorry. I can't believe I
told you to go. It's the last thing I want.'

Sarah glanced around the unit. The staff were all
preoccupied but she lowered her voice anyway.
'It's the last thing I want, too, Paul.'

'I was upset. I couldn't believe Daniel would be
so anti.'

'How is Daniel?'

Paul sighed heavily. 'We've had a long talk. I tried to reassure him. Tried to explain that my loving you didn't mean I loved him any less. I also tried to explain that not having you in my life would make me very unhappy and that wouldn't help my relationship with him.'

'How did he react to that?'

'He was pretty quiet. I guess he needs a bit of time to adjust to the idea. He's asked me to read him a bedtime story. He's done that for himself for a long time now so I think he's still upset.'

Sarah's beeper sounded. 'I'd better answer that,' she said apologetically. 'Can I call you back?'

'I'd really like that.' The warmth of the response flowed through Sarah as she replaced the handpiece and immediately lifted it again to dial the number on her pager. In response to that call Sarah hurried down to Emergency. A ten-day-old baby had been rushed in, after being found not breathing and blue in his bassinet. Resuscitation attempts had been successful and Sarah found no evidence of any abnormality when she carefully examined the baby.

'Has he been unwell at all in the last few days?'

The baby's mother was pale. She shook her head.

'Is this your first baby?'

The young woman nodded. She held tightly to her husband's hand and it was he who answered Sarah's queries about the pregnancy and delivery. All had been normal.

'What position was he sleeping in?'

'On his back. We knew about not letting him

sleep on his stomach and not having a sheepskin. We thought we were doing all the right things.'

'I'm sure you were,' Sarah assured them. 'We can't explain why this happens in a lot of cases.'

'If we hadn't checked on him...' The mother's voice was a terrified whisper.

'It's very lucky that you did.' Sarah wrapped the baby back in its shawl and placed him in his mother's arms. 'We'll keep George in tonight and monitor his breathing. We'll be able to check him more thoroughly tomorrow as well.'

'What about after that?' George's father spoke up again. 'Wendy was nervous enough as a new mother before this. We'll never get any sleep now.'

'We can discuss the use of an apnoea monitor at home if necessary,' Sarah told him. 'They can be a hassle and cause stress with false alarms, but in view of this attack you might be happier to use one, at least for the next few months.'

'Will it stop it happening again?' George's mother looked hopeful.

'It doesn't prevent a baby from having an episode of not breathing,' Sarah said carefully. 'What it does do is give you a warning so that you can respond.' She smiled at the parents. 'You responded very well in this case and George seems fine. Let's get you up to the ward. The nursing staff can show you the monitors and discuss it with you again.'

Sarah tried to ring Paul back, having seen George up to the ward, but there was no answer. Puzzled, she let the phone ring and ring.

'It must be a good book,' she decided finally, replacing the receiver. Heading back to the neonatal unit, Sarah realised she'd left her stethoscope in Emergency. Her beeper sounded as soon as she'd retraced her path.

'Sarah?'

'Paul. What's wrong?' She had recognised the voice, but only just. He sounded terrible. 'What's happened?' Sarah cried.

'It's Daniel.' Paul seemed to be catching his breath. 'He's run away.'

'What?' Sarah was shocked. 'Are you sure?'

'I went to read him a story and he wasn't in his room. I've checked the building, and Mrs Henry's and the garage.' There was a moment's heavy silence. 'I've just called the police.'

'Oh, God,' Sarah breathed.

Beside the wall phone Sarah was using was the desk on which stood a radio transmitter. It was the contact point between the department and the ambulance service. It warned the department of incoming casualties and their status, and also allowed medical advice to be given to paramedics, attending an accident scene. It crackled into life as Sarah clutched the phone. A senior nurse depressed the button on the microphone.

'Emergency here, Ambulance Three.'

'We're attending a hit-and-run accident, involving a boy approximately eight to ten years old. Serious head injury, unconscious. Please advise on airway control.'

Sarah covered the mouthpiece of the telephone. 'What street is it in?' she asked urgently. The nurse looked up at her sharply but passed the microphone to the registrar on duty, Matt Warnock.

'Please,' Sarah begged. 'What street?'

'Sarah?' She could hear a frantic note in Paul's voice. 'Sarah? Are you still there?'

'Hang on, Paul.' Sarah covered the phone again. Matt paused in his queries about the child's vital signs. 'Worcester Street,' he told her tersely.

'Paul? Are you anywhere near Worcester Street?'

'It's just around the corner. What—?'

'There's an ambulance attending an accident,' Sarah said carefully. 'It probably isn't Daniel, but—'

There was nothing more she could say. Sarah could hear the thump of the dropped handpiece as it swung against the wall. A few seconds later came the tone of a disconnected call. Sarah hung up at her end and tuned in to the instructions the registrar was issuing.

'Do you have an oral airway in place?'

'Affirmative.'

'Ventilate by mask. Have you got IV access?'

'Working on it now.'

'Make sure it's wide bore. Use one third normal saline. Let half a litre run in fast. Put on a cervical collar and use a spinal board. What's your ETA?'

'About ten minutes.'

Sarah closed her eyes. Don't let it be Daniel, she begged silently.

But she knew.

She knew it couldn't be anyone else.

CHAPTER SEVEN

IT WAS the longest ten minutes of Sarah Kendall's life.

The identity of the young hit-and-run victim had been confirmed when Paul arrived at the accident scene just as they were transferring Daniel to the ambulance. Matt took one look at Sarah's face and contacted another paediatric registrar on duty to arrange cover for the neonatal unit. He contacted the neurosurgical registrar on take, an anaesthetist and the X-ray department. The high status number and the triple 8 code given by the paramedic staff had been a priority signal to get the appropriate specialists and equipment to Emergency.

'We need a portable unit in Emergency and have the CT scan staff on standby,' he ordered. 'We've got a young accident victim on the way in with multiple injuries, including a compound, depressed skull fracture.'

Sarah shuddered. It had been Paul who'd examined Daniel in the ambulance and made the diagnosis of the head injury. Sarah had never felt so afraid in her life. Would Daniel even make it to the hospital? If he survived, was he going to have terrible brain damage? She knew Paul would blame himself. What if he also blamed their relationship—or her?

Sarah watched as the staff prepared the resusci-

tation room, IV, X-ray and cardiac monitoring
equipment. She could do nothing to help. It was
almost surreal, this waiting period. Medical staff
from the various specialties were gathering as the
wail of the siren was heard in the distance. Her own
fears had to be forgotten. Right now it was only
Daniel who mattered.

She ran with Matt and the triage nurse to help
lift out the stretcher as the ambulance doors swung
open. Then reality hit as she saw the small head
swathed in a blood-soaked dressing, the airway dis-
torting the mouth and the paramedic holding the
ambu-bag. She looked at the end of the stretcher
where the portable cardiac monitor showed an er-
ratic trace and then to the other end where the bag
of IV fluid was being held aloft by a white-faced
Paul. The moment seemed suspended in time and
then suddenly Sarah found it easy to forget about
herself totally as controlled chaos broke out.

They took the stretcher at a run to the resuscitation room. Four people arranged themselves instantly on either side.

'On the count of three. One, two...'

They lifted the small body, gently transferring it
onto the bed with the least possible movement to
the head and neck. Sarah could only stand and
watch as the team of medical staff went to work.
The anaesthetist took over the airway, suctioning
out secretions. The neurosurgical registrar checked
pupils and reflexes, calling to Daniel to try and get
a response. Daniel's clothes were being cut away
by a nurse. Another was replacing ECG leads and
taking blood pressure. Matt was inserting a second

IV line. It seemed as if everyone w̶
once.

'Any CSF leaking from the nose or ea̶

'Fifty percent oxygen.'

'We need bloods for CBC, electrolytes,
lase…'

'Do an arterial puncture for blood gas…'

'Type and crossmatch. We need units here
now—he's losing a lot of blood. Start some haemaccel, stat—'

Sarah pressed herself further into the corner as
the staff moved rapidly. She watched in horror as
the dressing from Daniel's head was removed and
fresh blood covered the gloved hands of the neurosurgical registrar, gently examining him. She had
to move again as the bulky X-ray machine was
pushed in. The orders still flowed.

'Skull, cervical spine, chest and pelvis shots.'
The X-ray technicians joined the throng of staff.

'He's bleeding from somewhere else. This scalp
wound isn't enough for that drop.'

'Has he got a gag reflex?'

'Yes. Pass me that nasogastric tube.'

'Four broken ribs, right side.'

'What's the blood pressure?'

'What's the Glasgow coma scale score?'

Sarah found the sounds blurring. She could still
hear people calling to Daniel, trying to elicit some
sort of response.

'No eye opening—pupils dilated.'

'No verbal response.'

'Minimal flexion to pain. GCS score of five.

anaesthetist's orders took

nal anaesthesia if we can
m into refractory shock.
cious. Give me some
we'll go for a crash

ax here, thanks to these
advised.

explains the extra blood loss, then. We'll
do an intercostal drain as soon as we've got him
ventilated. Somebody booked a CT scan?'

'Blood pressure's dropping—unreadable,' a
nurse warned.

'Tachycardia!' Someone else advised. 'No, ventricular fibrillation.'

'He's arresting!'

The X-ray staff and several others backed away
as the activity became frantic. Sarah knew she
shouldn't really be there. She was only a spectator.
But she wasn't watching alone. Her hand had lost
all feeling due to the vice-like grip in which it was
being held. She wasn't sure who turned away first
as the CPR began on Daniel but she clung to Paul
and held him, hoping somehow to drive away the
horror of what was happening. She felt the man in
her arms cringe as they heard the discharge of the
defibrillator.

'Sinus rhythm.'

The sigh of relief was collective but it was several seconds before Sarah and Paul turned back to
the scene. Gradually, the staff completed their urgent investigations and the ventilation procedures

were finished. A more controlled atmosphere descended and Matt finally left Daniel's side and came over to Paul.

His smile acknowledged the grim situation. 'We're over the first hurdle.' He tried to sound encouraging. 'He's stable for the moment.' He glanced back at Daniel, frowning. 'He's got severe bruising on his right leg but no fractures. The broken ribs caused a haemothorax—we've drained a good half-litre of blood from his chest and shouldn't need to treat that any further. Pelvis is OK and no sign of abdominal haemorrhage. The most serious injury is obviously the skull fractures and we're going to take him up for a CT head now.'

'Fractures?' Sarah had not picked up that there was more than one.

'He's got the depressed, compound fracture on top and another fracture at the base,' Matt told her. 'That one doesn't look too serious but I expect he'll have a couple of pretty black eyes. Anyway, the scan will tell us a bit more so let's get this show on the road.'

Paul nodded grimly. Sarah kept a tight hold of his hand as they trailed after the bed and attendant staff. They had both been in this situation many times but never on the receiving end. The change in perspective was total. And terrifying. Despite her own knowledge and experience, Sarah felt helpless, totally dependent on the professional staff around them. If she felt like this, she could only imagine what Paul was going through. Being able to interpret the test results and understand the language and procedures didn't make it any easier. In some ways it made the situation worse.

The CT scan was performed quickly. Sarah watched silently as Daniel's tiny form disappeared into the circular opening of the huge machine. She watched Paul's face as his eyes, darker than she had ever seen them, were riveted to the screens, displaying the images. His voice, as he discussed what they were seeing with the radiologist and surgeon, was hoarse with strain.

'Dual fractures. I'm more concerned with this compound one.'

'We've got some cerebral contusion and haematoma here...and here.'

'Doesn't look too extensive.'

'It's well away from the motor complex. That should reduce the risk of seizures.'

'We'll still need a loading dose of anticonvulsants prior to surgery.'

'When will you operate?'

'Immediately. I want to relieve those haematomas and elevate the depressed fracture. We'll have to repair the dura as well but it doesn't look too bad.' The surgeon laid his hand on Paul's shoulder. 'We'll start antistaphylococcal antibiotics immediately. We should be in Theatre within an hour. It's looking pretty manageable from where I'm standing at present.'

Sarah and Paul stayed with Daniel until he was taken to Theatre. Suddenly, after all the intensive activity and all the people around them, they were left alone.

'Let's get some fresh air,' Sarah suggested.

Paul shook his head. They were in the theatre reception area. Paul's request to observe the surgery had been gently but firmly refused by the surgeon, much to Sarah's relief. He was a parent right now, not a surgeon—ex or otherwise. The theatre was no place for him to be. She took his hand and led him to the theatre staff's common room, deserted at present thanks to their emergency and a Caesarean in the adjoining theatre.

'Sit down,' she ordered. 'I'll make us some coffee.' She went to hand Paul a mug of the steaming liquid but he had his face buried in his hands.

'This is all my fault,' Paul groaned. 'I'll never forgive myself if...if...' His voice faded. The end of the thought was unbearable.

Sarah put both mugs down on the table and sat beside Paul. 'I'm to blame just as much as you are, Paul.'

'Don't be ridiculous.' Paul's chair was pushed back with a harsh scrape. He jerked to his feet and began to pace around the small room. 'I was the one who pushed it. I insisted on our engagement. I was determined to tell Daniel about it. I had to have what *I* wanted so badly. Never mind my son.'

'You've done everything you could for Daniel,' Sarah stated firmly. 'For God's sake, Paul, you've brought him up entirely by yourself. You've thrown away a career you loved just so you could be there to take him to school in the mornings, read to him at night, spend the weekends with him. You've given him all the love and security he could need.'

'Not enough.' Paul's voice was agonised. 'You said yourself he wasn't secure enough to share my love. No wonder he felt he wasn't important any more. That he had to run away to try and show me how much he mattered. How could I have been so bloody selfish?'

'Don't make it an evil thing that we fell in love, Paul.' Sarah struggled against tears. The stress of their situation was being made so much worse by watching the man she loved, tearing himself to pieces. 'Please!'

Paul stopped pacing. He threw himself back into his chair. 'I'm not,' he said brokenly. 'It's just— I'm torn apart, Sarah. I love my son but I didn't love him enough. I should have known how he felt. I wasn't prepared to give you up for his sake, even temporarily. And now, if he...' Paul drew in a long shuddering breath. 'If he doesn't make it how can we live with the fact that it was our relationship that was responsible? I'm in a totally no-win situation here, Sarah, and it's killing me.'

'Would you rather I wasn't here?' Sarah spoke quietly, ignoring the tears that escaped and rolled down her cheeks.

'No. God, no.' Paul reached out and took Sarah's hand in both of his. 'You're the only lifeline I've got right now. Don't leave me.'

Sarah's lips trembled. 'I'm not going to leave, Paul. Not unless you want me to.'

'If anybody's to blame it's the driver of that car!' Paul's voice rose in anger. 'Did you know he stopped and then took off? The bastard!' Paul let go of Sarah's hand and his fist crashed onto the table. 'How could anybody do that? To a child...' He stared, unseeing, at the spilled coffee. 'Thank

God there was a witness. If the ambulance hadn't got there so fast...'

'Did they get a licence number?'

'No. Male driver. A late model Japanese car of some description. Black.'

'No wonder Daniel didn't see it.'

'He wasn't looking.' Paul rubbed his forehead with his palm. 'He was too upset to think about looking.'

'Mr Henderson?'

Sarah and Paul both jumped and then froze. Sarah found she couldn't breathe as she waited for the nurse to speak. How long had they been in here? It seemed too soon for news. How could it be anything but bad?

'Daniel's in Recovery now. Would you like to come and see him?'

The small boy looked peacefully asleep. The dressings to his head were a pristine contrast to the blood-soaked dressing they had last seen. Sarah listened quietly as the surgeon explained the situation to Paul.

'Very straightforward. We elevated and debrided the bone fragments and repaired the dural lacerations. Minimal extradural and subdural haematomas which we've cleaned up. We'll continue the prophylactic anticonvulsants. We've got an ICP monitor inserted.' The surgeon pointed to a probe, coming through the bandaging on Daniel's head. Sarah looked at the monitor reading as she heard the surgeon discussing the dosage of steroids and diuretics he was planning. A rise in intracranial pressure would signify what Daniel was now most at risk of—the development of acute brain swelling.

'We've got arterial and Swan-Ganz catheters in,' the surgeon continued. 'I want to keep a close eye on pressures and cardiac output for the moment. We'll keep hyperventilation going and monitor respiratory function, and he's got a urinary catheter in place. We need to keep an accurate fluid balance and watch renal function. These lines here...' he touched the plastic ports attached to another catheter in Daniel's arm '...are for serial blood sampling. That one's for IV drug administration and for fluids, which are at two thirds maintenance at present.'

Paul nodded.

'Any questions?' He looked at Paul and then raised an eyebrow at Sarah. 'No? We'll make a move to ICU, then. I'll see you shortly.' The surgeon made a final check of Daniel's pupil reaction. 'We'll reduce the sedation tomorrow but I can't say when he'll regain consciousness. So far he's doing as well as we could hope for.'

It was in the early hours of the morning before Daniel was settled in the intensive care unit. A comfortable armchair was placed alongside his bed for Paul. Sarah felt suddenly out of place.

'Do you want me to stay?'

Paul's face held only the hint of a smile as he looked at her. The lines around his eyes were deeply etched, the shadows beneath them mirrored by the dark roughness of his unshaven beard. He looked exhausted and desperately unhappy. Sarah touched the roughness of his cheek.

'You're going to need a razor and a change of clothes. I'll go and get them for you.'

'Thanks.' Paul caught her hand and pressed it against his cheek for a moment. The gesture conveyed all Sarah needed to know.

'Have you got your key?'

Paul shook his head. 'I didn't stop to lock up.'

Sarah nodded. 'I'll fix it. Is there anything special of Daniel's you'd like me to bring? For when he wakes up?'

Paul's eyes thanked her for her optimism. He sighed heavily. 'I can't think. Oh, wait. There's a book he always reads—an encyclopaedia of dogs—and there's an old toy, a kind of dog thing with black spots. He's had it since he was a baby.' Paul's voice had a harsh edge to it. 'One of the only things his mother ever gave him. God knows why he kept it.' He pressed his lips together and shut his eyes, as though blotting out a memory or perhaps the present situation.

'I'll find it,' Sarah promised. 'I'll be back as soon as I can.'

'You should get some sleep,' Paul said heavily. 'There's no rush. We're not going anywhere.'

Sarah did manage a couple of hours of troubled sleep just before dawn. Daniel was stable and Paul was by his side. It was a vigil Sarah was unable to share completely, either in time or emotionally. She was, however, not in good shape when she arrived for duty on Ward 23.

'What on earth's the matter?' Angela and Judith fussed around Sarah. If they noticed the fact that her engagement ring was now missing they said nothing. Sarah was still explaining the situation, somewhat tearfully, when Martin Lynch entered the office.

'I read about the accident,' he told Sarah. 'It's front-page news. You shouldn't be here.'

'I need to do something,' Sarah protested. 'The waiting is so hard.'

'You're in no condition to treat anybody.' Martin Lynch gripped Sarah's shoulder. 'You need some food and some rest and to be there when they need you.' He smiled at her kindly. 'They're your family-to-be.'

Angela and Judith made noises of agreement. 'Everything's under control here,' Angela assured Sarah. 'Even Anthony's IV line is still in.'

Sarah smiled lopsidedly. 'I knew he wouldn't get that one out.'

'Go,' Martin Lynch ordered. 'There's only a few days of your run left and I'll see it covered. We don't want to see you back here unless you're handing out wedding invitations.'

If only they knew, Sarah thought miserably as she left the ward, how unlikely that now was. Paul had said he was in a no-win situation. She felt that she was also in it—even deeper. If Daniel survived and Paul broke off their relationship at least he would have his son. Sarah would have no one.

That's not entirely true, she reminded herself. Starting her car, she found herself heading out of the city. She still had her family and right now that was where she needed to be. She rang Paul as soon as she got there. The situation was unchanged.

'I've still got your key. I'll get another change of clothes for you and come in this evening. Ring me if there's any news.'

'Get some sleep, Sarah. One of us needs to.'

'I will. I'll watch Daniel tonight so you can get some, too.'

There was a silence. Sarah could feel the despair at the other end of the line. 'Paul?'

'Yes.'

'Don't give up. On anything.'

Not giving up was also the message Sarah's parents gave her repeatedly. Her mother's optimism, good food and care for her well-being was enhanced by her father's practical advice and encouragement. Sarah felt rested and greatly cheered by the time she arrived back at the hospital. She found Paul reading to Daniel from the encyclopaedia of dogs.

'"Road exercise on a lead is important for all dogs,"' she heard. '"It is essential to harden the pads of the feet, strengthen the toes and keep the nails short."'. Paul stopped and looked up as Sarah approached. He smiled ruefully.

'I ran out of things to talk about. I doubt if he can even hear me, anyway.'

They both looked at the unconscious child. The bruising around his eyes had darkened dramatically, giving him a racoon-like mask. The rings were made all the more dramatic by the contrast they made with the white bandaging and his pale skin.

The rhythmic click and hiss of the ventilator and the bleeps of various monitors filled the silence.

'You don't know that,' Sarah said. 'Even if he can't respond, some part of his brain might be aware of your presence and the sound of your voice.'

'That's what I keep telling myself.' Paul sighed. 'Has he shown any signs of waking up?'

'There's some spontaneous respiration,' Paul told her. 'That's about all. Cardiac function is stable. They've taken out the Swan-Ganz line.'

'That's a start.' Sarah looked at all the other lines still attached to Daniel. There was a fair way to go.

Paul followed her gaze. Then he took hold of her hand. 'I'm glad you're here, Sarah.'

'So am I.' Sarah looked at Paul with concern. He obviously hadn't used the razor she'd brought him. If he'd changed his shirt that wasn't apparent either. The rolled-up sleeves and sweat stains made him look even more exhausted. 'You need to have a shower and shave,' she told him firmly. 'And to get into some clean clothes.'

'No. I can't leave him.'

'It's only for ten minutes, Paul. You'll be a lot more use to him if you're feeling better. I'll be here.'

Eventually Sarah persuaded him and he did look refreshed when he returned. He refused to go out for food, however, so Sarah collected dinner on a tray from the cafeteria and carried it back. He also refused to sleep, despite Sarah being there to watch Daniel, but exhaustion finally took its toll and Paul fell asleep in the armchair. Sarah covered him with a blanket and sat on another chair close to the bed.

Nursing staff came and went unobtrusively. They changed Daniel's position and checked his skin condition, suctioned the airway and checked the respirator tubing connections. One nurse came to put artificial tears in his eyes, another to take blood and urine samples. Recordings of measurements and observations were added to frequently. But Sarah felt mostly alone. She watched the monitors, watched Paul sleeping and watched Daniel's still face. She took hold of one of the boy's hands and just sat, quietly holding it, not speaking or moving.

Sarah became aware of the warmth of the small hand and felt it gradually flow into herself. At some point during the lonely vigil Sarah became acutely aware of the love she now felt for this child—not just because he was a part of the man she loved so deeply but just because he was Daniel. A small boy who had been betrayed by his mother and was lonely for the love he should have had from her. A child, like his father, who was passionate about the things important to him and desperately sensitive and vulnerable.

Sarah wanted more than anything to enfold this child, to make everything all right and to let him know how much she loved him. She wondered at her own intense reaction. This must be how mothers feel, she thought, and she felt a slow tear trickle down her cheek.

Paul slept for several hours but couldn't be persuaded to leave Daniel for fresh air or breakfast. By dinnertime that day, however, he was ready for a break. Sarah was worried about his emotional state. They were in a kind of limbo that could only be broken when Daniel regained consciousness. So far he had shown no signs of doing so. A repeat CT scan that day had been promising. All his vital signs were stable and he was being successfully weaned from the ventilator. His breathing had been stable enough to take him off the machine for long periods, leaving him to breathe through the endotracheal tube.

When the coma showed signs of further lightening they would then remove the tube to let him breathe unassisted. There was even some response to painful stimuli, such as eyebrow pinching, but still he wouldn't wake up.

Throughout another long night and day they held on. The media interest in the story continued. The hunt for the driver of the car escalated. Paul was interviewed by the police. The driver had been aware of the accident and it was possible he had returned to observe the aftermath. Had Paul noticed anything? There had been onlookers but he had been aware of no one but his son. Now his only concern was for Daniel's welfare. He couldn't help.

He refused interviews with the media who now listed Daniel's condition as serious but stable and concentrated their attention on the police operation to narrow and trace the make of car involved. Cards, flowers and gifts from well-wishers poured into the hospital. Most had to be stored away from Daniel's area in the intensive care unit.

Paul became more easily persuaded to leave his son's bedside for short intervals. By the evening of the fourth day Sarah was seriously worried. Despite the strength Paul showed and shared with her, she sensed in him a desperation that seemed close to breaking point.

She watched him pick at a meal in the cafeteria and then they walked by the river. Sarah noticed how often his eyes flicked down to the pager she was still carrying, despite having finished her hospital duties. He expected, and at the same time dreaded, a summons. Still, they talked. Not about Daniel. The long hours they were sharing together had provided an opportunity to really talk—about themselves.

They discussed their families, their childhoods and schooling, their dreams. Sarah felt she finally knew this man she had fallen in love with, and the knowledge only served to increase that love. The only thing they didn't discuss was marriage. Underlying much of what Paul said was the commitment he felt to his son and the priority he now gave their relationship. Sarah was too afraid to find out how she now fitted in.

Another topic they avoided was Daniel's mother, Catherine. Although curious, Sarah was quite content to wait until Paul felt ready to tell her about his ex-wife. It would not be that evening, however. When Sarah's pager sounded they both looked at each other in alarm. Hand in hand, they ran back towards the hospital, taking the stairs rather than waiting for a lift. When they saw the two police officers outside the doors to the intensive care unit they both slowed and then stopped, paralysed by a mutual fear.

Had the intensive police operation to find the hit-and-run driver now become a homicide inquiry?

CHAPTER EIGHT

'He's been arrested.'

'Who?' Paul seemed bewildered and Sarah knew the stress and exhaustion were taking a greater toll on him than she had feared.

'The hit-and-run driver,' the police office explained. 'He came forward finally. We thought you'd like to know.'

'Not really.' Paul began to walk towards the ICU doors. 'I've got my only child lying in a coma. That's the only thing I'm interested in.'

The police officers looked embarrassed. 'He was a teenager,' one said to Sarah. 'He panicked. Apparently, he returned to the scene shortly afterwards but saw that help had already arrived. He's very upset about it all.'

Sarah nodded. 'I'm sure he is. But, as Mr Henderson said, Daniel is our only concern right now. Excuse me.'

Sarah expected to find Paul in his usual position, holding Daniel's hand and talking to him. Instead she found him slumped in the armchair, his face buried in his hands. She touched his shoulders gently.

'I don't know how much longer I can take this.' His voice was muffled but Sarah could hear the pain only too well. She wasn't sure what she said to try and comfort him but the words kept flowing as she

tried gently to massage some of the strain from
Paul's shoulders and neck. She was also not sure at
what point he fell asleep but she covered him with
a blanket and sighed with relief.

For a long time Sarah sat and watched Daniel.
She held his hand and talked quietly, willing his
fingers to twitch or the dark lashes against his
cheeks to flutter. The tube had been removed that
afternoon. Daniel's breathing was strong and
steady. The severe bruising around his eyes was
fading now, and he looked as though he were
merely asleep, the scruffy soft toy dog, so obviously
treasured, tucked in beside him.

'It's time to wake up now, Daniel,' Sarah said
softly.

The nurse who came in to check the equipment
at that point smiled sympathetically at Sarah. 'He
will,' she said encouragingly. 'The EKG was definitely picking up today. He's showing response to
stimuli and commands. It's just not voluntary yet.
He just needs a good incentive,' she added. 'It
won't be much longer.'

'It's already been too long,' Sarah said, glancing
over her shoulder at Paul. Even in sleep his face
looked grim, the deeply shadowed eyes and downward curve of his lips testimony to his emotional
trauma. She looked back at Daniel and then at the
nurse.

'I've got an idea,' she said slowly. 'I'm going to
need your help, though. And I need to make a few
phone calls.'

It was just over an hour later that Sarah was again
at Daniel's bedside. The nurse looked up from her

seat beside the bed. 'No change,' she reported and then smiled. 'In either of them.' She glanced at Paul. 'Did you get permission?'

Sarah nodded, biting her bottom lip as she smiled. One arm had been tucked inside her coat. She now pulled the garment open with her other hand to show the nurse what she held.

'I'll leave you to it,' the nurse said. 'Good luck.'

Sarah took a deep breath and sat on the edge of Daniel's bed. It had been one thing to take a duckling into a general paediatric ward but this was something much more serious, and approval had been given only grudgingly by the consultant. She didn't have much time. Carefully, she took the six-week-old retriever puppy and sat him on the bed beside Daniel's hand. She stroked it gently.

'Behave yourself,' she whispered sternly, 'or we'll both be in big trouble.' Raising her voice a little, Sarah spoke to Daniel.

'You've got a visitor, Daniel. His name is Luke.' She picked up Daniel's limp hand and, holding it in her own, stroked it over the puppy. 'He's one of the babies you've already met. Do you remember? Feel how soft he is. Can you feel his ears?' Luke obligingly licked Daniel's fingers and Sarah was careful to protect the IV line going into the back of his hand. She kept talking. 'Luke really likes you, Daniel. He'd really like you to say hello to him.'

There was no discernible response from the child and gradually Sarah fell silent. It had seemed like such a wonderful idea but it wasn't going to make any difference at all. Tired out from his late night adventure, Luke curled up and went to sleep. Sarah's eyes also drooped. She'd just rest for a minute and then she'd have to put the puppy back in the box in her car.

Her eyes jerked open when she felt a touch on her cheek. She found Paul, smiling, and her own lips curved in an instant response. She hadn't seen Paul really smile since the accident happened and she'd forgotten the warmth it created in her.

'It was a brilliant idea,' he murmured.

'It would have been—if it had worked.' Sarah's smile faded and she looked down. The puppy was still asleep, Daniel's hand resting on its back.

'Paul?'

'Yes, my love?' Paul was still watching Sarah, his hand now stroking her neck.

'Is it my imagination?'

'What's that?'

'That Daniel's fingers just moved.'

The hand froze on her neck. Sarah held her breath. She was genuinely unsure of what she'd seen. Perhaps it had been wishful thinking and maybe she was unwarranted in raising Paul's hopes. They both watched, transfixed, as Daniel's hand moved infinitely slowly towards the head of the puppy. As it began to track down the puppy's back again Sarah saw the flutter of eyelashes. Carefully, she eased herself off the bed and backed away. She didn't want to be the first person Daniel saw if he opened his eyes. She didn't see the actual moment it happened but she was still close enough to hear Daniel's first mumbled words.

'Hi, Dad. Is Luke going to be my puppy?'

There could have been no better indication that Daniel was going to be all right and that no serious brain damage had been sustained.

He remained in the intensive care unit for another two days and was then transferred to Sarah's old haunt, Ward 23. Angela and Judith promised to take special care of their new addition and even agreed to another smuggled visit by Luke. Sarah had deliberately kept a low profile since Daniel had come out of his coma and Paul hadn't objected—somewhat to her dismay.

'I'm reluctant to push anything just now,' he'd explained. 'I nearly lost my son and it's made me think hard about our future.'

Whose future? Sarah wondered. Paul and Daniel's or Paul's and her own? But Paul was happier to spend more time away from Daniel now. He had some urgent duties to attend to as manager but the rest of the time he spent with Sarah. They'd made love for the first time in over a week the night after Daniel had been transferred to the ward. It had been a time of exquisite gentleness—an act of healing as much as of passion. Life seemed to be beginning again but the emphasis had changed. Daniel's well-being still held top priority.

'He's been asking to see Luke again,' Paul told Sarah. 'I told him that it was up to you. That it had been your idea in the first place.'

Sarah nodded. 'I did have some help. The staff had to agree and Mum met me halfway to town with the puppy. Perhaps I should get Mum to visit him with Luke.'

'He'd like to see your mum,' Paul agreed, 'but I think you should bring the puppy in yourself.'

Sarah had to laugh. 'And I thought I was the only child psychologist around here.'

The visit was a huge success, despite the fact that Luke wet Daniel's bed and chewed up three get well cards. Sarah and Daniel talked dogs and Daniel's eyes were shining by the end of the visit, but he did look very tired.

'Dad said maybe I would be able to keep Luke, Sarah. Do you think it would be all right with your mum?'

'I'll let you talk to her about that yourself. She's going to come and visit you soon. But I'll tell her not to sell him to anybody.'

'Thanks, Sarah.' Daniel yawned. Sarah scooped up Luke and put him back in his box.

'I'll get Judith to bring you some clean sheets.' She smiled. 'Maybe next time we'd better play with Luke outside.'

It was an unusual few days for Sarah. She spent a lot of time in Ward 23 but not as a doctor. Daniel's recovery was proceeding well, though he still suffered from bad headaches and tired very easily. Cheryl was working with him daily to mobilise and strengthen his badly bruised leg.

Sarah was sitting with Daniel one afternoon during the rest period when the physiotherapist poked her head around the door. Daniel groaned when he saw her.

'Oh, no. Not again! We're busy.' Daniel waved at the mess on his bed. They were sifting through a stack of old magazines, cutting out all the pictures of dogs they could find.

'We've done your work for today.' Cheryl smiled. 'It was Sarah I was hoping to find. I've got someone who's very keen to say hello.' She stepped back and Michael eased into view. He was carrying the soccer ball under his arm.

'Hey, Michael!' Sarah was delighted to see him. 'Are you ready for that game?'

'Yeah.'

'I'll be right there. This is Daniel. Daniel—this is my friend, Michael.' Sarah turned to Daniel as she made the introduction and was surprised to find him scowling suspiciously.

'Sarah's visiting *me*,' he informed Michael.

Sarah suppressed more than a smile. The jealousy was almost palpable. For the first time Sarah felt she had won a place in Daniel's heart. He was responding to her love and that could only mean an assurance of what she desperately craved for her own future.

'Tell you what, Daniel. Let's put you in a wheelchair and you can come and help me play soccer with Michael. Would you like to be goalie?'

The scowl faded. 'Can I be on your goal?'

Sarah couldn't wait to tell Paul. She knew he was having meetings all afternoon to finalise new contract details with the cleaners' union. The stalemate had been broken while Daniel had been in his coma. Paul had been completely disinterested and Sarah knew he wouldn't have gained any satisfaction from bickering over any final details today.

Even so, she was surprised to find him looking so grim when she went to his office after five.

'How did it go?'

'I gave them pretty much what they wanted on the minor issues. They're happy.'

'So it's all settled?'

Paul nodded. He drummed his fingers on his desk. Sarah noticed how dark his eyes were and could find no hint of a smile when she searched his face.

'But there's still a problem?'

He nodded again.

'Are you going to tell me about it?'

Paul picked up the fax that he had been drumming his fingers on. He waved it in the air and then slapped it back onto the desk angrily.

'This message is from Catherine. My ex-wife,' he explained, as though Sarah might have forgotten who she was. 'Thanks to the publicity surrounding Daniel's accident, some well-meaning old friend decided she should know about it.'

'And?' Sarah sensed there was more to Paul's anger. Much more.

'She's planning to visit him. Arriving the day after tomorrow.'

'From where?'

'Washington, D.C. I have the flight details here.'

'How do you think Daniel will react?'

'I have no idea. But I'm about to find out.' Paul jerked to his feet. 'This is the last thing we need.'

Sarah nodded. The triumph of her breakthrough with Daniel that afternoon suddenly lost its significance. How could she compte with a 'real' mother?

'And that's not all,' Paul sighed angrily. 'She's informed me in this communication that she's planning to sue for custody of Daniel.'

'What?' Sarah's mouth dropped open.

'It's all couched in legal terms. Basically it says if I can't ensure the child's safety then I must be an unfit parent. She's going to take over the rest of his upbringing and can do it much more to his advantage, thanks to her stable remarriage, permanent house staff and position in society earned by a very successful career in law.'

'She hasn't got a prayer,' Sarah hissed. 'She abandoned him as a baby, for God's sake.'

'Eight-year-olds are much less demanding than babies,' Paul said bitterly, 'and much less likely to interfere with career ambitions. Especially when you can afford to pay other people to raise the child.' Paul screwed his eyes shut as he rubbed his face. 'Unfortunately, my solicitor thinks she has a case, particularly in view of the fact that I'm not providing what might be considered a nuclear family situation.'

'Meaning?'

'That I'm not married. He has no mother figure in his life.'

'Yes, he does,' Sarah argued. 'Me.'

Paul rested both hands on Sarah's shoulders. 'That isn't enough. Not yet. We're not married.'

'In the words of someone I know rather well...' Sarah smiled faintly. 'That can be arranged.'

Paul's grip on her shoulders tightened. 'You'd do that? You'd marry me to give me grounds to fight this custody case?'

Sarah looked him squarely in the eye. 'No, Paul. I'd do that because I love you. Because I also love Daniel. And especially because I'm not going to let anything—or anyone—destroy our future together.'

CHAPTER NINE

'I ALWAYS knew she'd come back. That's why I kept Spot.' Daniel was clutching the old soft toy excitedly. 'So she'd know I hadn't forgotten. How many hours is it now, Sarah?'

Sarah tried to smile. 'Sixteen,' she told him. If seemed that she'd been counting the hours for ever, but her anticipation of the event couldn't have been more different to Daniel's. She was dreading it. 'It's time you got some sleep. When you wake up it won't be long to wait.'

'I know.' Daniel sighed happily. 'Do you think she's missed me, Sarah?'

'I think she must be very concerned about you to be coming all this way,' Sarah said carefully. She began to straighten Daniel's bed. Paul had gone to find him a glass of water.

'Do you think she'll want to take me back with her?'

Daniel's query startled Sarah. Paul had told him only of the intended visit. No mention had been made of the bid for custody.

'That would mean leaving your dad,' she said quietly. 'I thought you guys were a team.'

'We are.' Daniel's face fell, then he brightened. 'He'd still have you, though, wouldn't he?'

'Oh, yes. He'd still have me.' Daniel made no objection as Sarah bent and kissed his forehead.

'But the team would be missing its most important member.'

'Who's the most important member?' Paul came in, carrying the glass of water.

Sarah looked at Daniel but it was clear he didn't want to discuss the matter any more.

'Are you going to be here in the morning, Dad? For when my mother gets here?'

'I'll be here.' Paul kissed his son. Then his gaze caught Sarah's and she read in him the same dread she felt enclosing herself. Once again their future seemed uncertain. Whatever the outcome of tomorrow's visit, the balance would be changed in some fashion. The rocky foundations of their lives at present seemed no base to be building on.

Catherine's flight was due in at ten a.m. the next day. Allowing for time to clear customs and get a taxi to the hospital, Catherine wasn't expected until at least eleven. Paul refused to meet his ex-wife at the airport.

'She wasn't invited. She's not wanted,' he said bitterly to Sarah. 'The sooner she gets that message the better.'

'Daniel seems to want her,' Sarah pointed out. 'He can think about nothing else.'

'Daniel wants a dream,' Paul said heavily. 'A fairy-tale ending to what he sees as the missing part of his life. When he meets Catherine that dream will be shattered. He won't find the love he craves. It never existed. She didn't want a baby. She refused to consider giving up her career, even for a few weeks. She wouldn't hear of breast-feeding. God, she wouldn't even hold him for three days.'

'Why did you marry her, Paul?'

'I'd known her for years. Off and on,' Paul said thoughtfully. 'I was nearly thirty. The initial drive for career success was beginning to fade. I recognised that I needed something more in my life. Catherine seemed to be in a similar position. She'd been made a partner in her law firm. She'd proved she could do it. Maybe she was ready for a new direction or maybe it was the idea that she was attracted to. It wasn't until she became pregnant that she realised it wasn't a choice she'd really considered. I had to work very hard to persuade her not to terminate the pregnancy. It was the beginning of the end as far as we were concerned.'

'So you don't think she really wants Daniel back?'

Paul snorted. 'Of course she doesn't. Perhaps it's an idea she's chasing again, without having considered the implications. Maybe she wants to have a final shot at me. Or maybe her conscience has been pricked at the reminder of the child she abandoned. Whatever her motives, I'm quite sure Daniel is going to end up hurt and I can't forgive her for that.'

'Perhaps it's something he has to go through,' Sarah suggested gently. 'While it's hard, not to be able to shield him from the pain, maybe it's necessary to heal an even greater hurt. All you can do is to be there for him. Help him through it and provide the security for him to build on afterwards.'

'Just like you're doing for me.' Paul smiled suddenly and Sarah felt his bitterness fade. 'What would I do without you, Sarah?'

'I hope you're never going to find out,' she replied seriously. 'Have you made the arrangements with the registry office?'

'Yes. Tomorrow at four.' Paul looked at Sarah with real concern. 'This isn't the way I wanted it to be, Sarah. For you—for us. Are you sure you don't want to invite your family?'

'No.' Sarah smiled wistfully. 'This is just between ourselves.' She laughed suddenly but without mirth. 'It's a bit ironic, isn't it?'

'Why?'

'You're seeing your ex-wife for the first time on the day you're going to remarry. Out with the old and in with the new?'

'Catherine was out of my life a very long time ago, Sarah. I just wish she'd stayed out. For Daniel's sake even more than my own.' Paul shook his head. Then he drew Sarah into his arms. 'And, just for the record, you're not ''new''. You've always been part of my life. It just took me a hell of a long time to find you.'

Sarah went shopping the next morning. It took her until well after eleven to find the dress she wanted to wear that afternoon. The soft apricot fabric was perfect for the autumn tones of her honey blonde hair and brown eyes. The simple design of the dress was casual but was transformed into elegance by the matching jacket. The accessories were easy to find but Sarah decided against a hat. A nearby florist provided a small bouquet of flowers in matching tones, making a buttonhole spray with the smallest blooms. Sarah had her hair trimmed and then took her purchases back to her flat.

It was now one o'clock and the tension she'd been trying to ignore became overriding. She rang Ward 23.

'Angela? It's me, Sarah. Is Daniel's mother still there with him?'

'No, she's not.'

Something in Angela's tone made Sarah catch her breath. 'What time did she leave? Is Daniel OK? Did she upset him?'

'No, Daniel's not OK and, yes, she did upset him. But not by what time she left.'

'Oh, God. What did she do?' Sarah felt suddenly cold. Angela sounded very angry.

'She didn't show up. That's what she did.'

'What do you mean? Is the flight delayed?' Sarah was bewildered.

'No. The flight was on time. She wasn't on it. Paul was here with Daniel, waiting. Paul rang the airport at eleven-thirty to check that the plane had come in on time. He rang again at twelve-thirty to find out whether she'd been on it. Apparently she didn't bother getting on at the other end.'

'Oh, no!' Sarah breathed. 'How's Daniel taking it?'

'He's not,' Angela replied shortly. 'He's sitting in a wheelchair, waiting, out by the lifts. He won't listen to anything anybody tells him. He's convinced she missed the flight and she'll be getting another one as soon as she can.'

'How's Paul?' Sarah was appalled at this turn of

events. How could that woman do this to her son? She had never even met Catherine but right now Sarah hated her.

'Worried. We all are. Daniel's overwrought. He didn't sleep much last night and was nearly sick with excitement all morning. It's hardly good for a recovering head-injury victim. We're considering giving him a hefty sedative right now.'

'I'm coming in,' Sarah told her friend. 'This is just awful!'

Sarah expected to find Daniel still watching the lift when she arrived but the area was deserted. The rest period was not yet over and the atmosphere of calm seemed inconsistent with the emotional trauma Sarah knew had occurred. She found Paul in Daniel's room. The curtains were closed and even in the dim light she could see that the small boy was deeply asleep. Paul and Sarah embraced fiercely and wordlessly. Then Paul led her out of the room and closed the door behind him.

'You heard, then?'

'I rang Angela. She said they were thinking of sedating him. I can't believe Catherine's done this to him, Paul.'

'I can,' Paul said harshly. 'It's all the proof needed that she couldn't care less about her son but Daniel won't—can't—accept that.'

A nurse approached the pair as they leaned against the wall by Daniel's door.

'Mr Henderson? Your secretary just rang. She says there's a fax for you from Washington. She thought you'd like to know.'

'Thanks.' Paul straightened his back. 'I'll go and

get it. I'm interested to see what excuse she's come up with.'

'Would you like me to stay with Daniel.'

'No. He'll sleep for hours. We gave him enough of a sedative to knock out a small elephant. Judith said she'll be watching him.'

'Then I'll come with you,' Sarah said decisively.

The fax was an excuse—of sorts. Catherine stated she had decided to wait until the custody hearing had been dealt with so that her visit could coincide with taking Daniel back to the States.

'Over my dead body,' Paul muttered.

Sarah sighed. 'Has any date been set for a preliminary hearing with the family court?'

'Early next week, according to my solicitor. He's keen to get a copy of our marriage certificate on his desk tomorrow.'

'Oh, Paul. How can we? After this?'

'How can we not?' Paul was watching Sarah carefully. 'Daniel's devastated, Sarah. Perhaps you were right when you said he needed to get through this in order to heal the greater hurt and build a future. But he's going to need a lot of help and I can't do it on my own.'

'I'm not sure he'll accept my help,' Sarah said nervously. 'We've achieved a friendship but that may not be enough. Even the trust he's built in me so far could well have been destroyed by what must seem like a new rejection from his mother.'

'I'm not talking about your helping Daniel precisely,' Paul said slowly. 'I said I couldn't do it on my own. It's me that needs you as well, Sarah.'

'But...' Sarah shook her head in confusion. She

sat down on the edge of Paul's desk. 'I thought that—because of the accident—your relationship with Daniel had priority, that you weren't going to jeopardise it by pushing him too far or too fast. I thought you were marrying me to make sure you win permanent custody.'

'No.' Paul almost shook Sarah when he gripped her shoulders. 'How could you think that? Sure, I might have been prepared to postpone our marriage if that would have helped. I thought I was being selfish. I blamed myself for Daniel's insecurity and unhappiness. But you know who is really to blame? His mother, that's who.' Paul's grip on Sarah's shoulders loosened. 'And I'm not being selfish in forcing you into Daniel's life. You know why?'

Sarah shook her head, her eyes fixed on Paul's so close to her own.

'When you're in an aeroplane and they're giving the safety demonstrations they show you how to use the oxygen masks, don't they?'

Sarah nodded, bemused by the turn in the conversation.

'You know what they say to any parents? That you have to attend to your own oxygen supply before you attend to the needs of your children. In order to help them you have to ensure that you're capable of doing it.' Paul's fingers traced the outline of Sarah's face. 'You're my oxygen supply. I can't help Daniel without you in my life, and he's going to need all the help I can give.'

'I'd like to help too,' Sarah whispered. 'Not just for you—or us—but because I love Daniel too.'

'I know you do.' Paul's smile was as gentle as

the fingers that now lingered on the curve of her lips. 'That night when he was still in the coma. You thought I was asleep but I woke for a while and watched you. You were holding his hand and crying. I didn't disturb you because I could feel I wasn't a part of that moment. I could also feel your love. I thought you looked like you were his mother.'

'I felt like it,' Sarah admitted shyly.

'One day Daniel will feel like your son,' Paul told her. 'I'm quite sure of it.'

'I wish he was.' Sarah bit her lip. 'I hope it's just a matter of love. And time.'

'Time!' Paul's eyes widened. He looked at his watch. 'We'll have to run. I've got my suit here but...' His gaze travelled over Sarah's jeans and her favourite Bart Simpson sweatshirt. 'Well, I guess it's quite appropriate in a way.'

Sarah laughed. 'We'll stop by my apartment. I can change in ten minutes. What about Daniel?'

'Judith has my cellphone number but I'm sure he'll sleep through till morning. You've no idea how done in he was.'

'I can imagine.' Sarah took the hand Paul offered her and climbed off the desk. 'We're not going to let it happen again.' She tugged his hand. 'Come on, we'd better not be late.'

The service was simple, the witnesses the registry office staff. Sarah experienced one moment of panic when the celebrant asked for the rings. She had completely forgotten the need for them. Paul produced a small velvet box from his suit pocket, inside which were two matching gold bands—his and hers.

'How did you manage to get the size so perfect?' Sarah queried afterwards. 'I'm impressed.'

'I knew you had a good reason to let me borrow your engagement ring.' Paul's smile was poignant. 'It let me have a matching wedding band made in the same size. That's why I didn't give it back straight away.'

'And I thought you were just glad to be released from your obligations.'

'Fat chance!' Paul's smile widened. He touched his glass to Sarah's. 'Here's to the future, Mrs Henderson.' He looked around them. 'I hope I can offer you a little more than this.'

Sarah grinned. 'Oh, I don't know. It's quite appropriate, really. I should have changed back into my sweatshirt and jeans.'

They were sitting on the floor of Paul's office in a deserted administration block. Fish and chip wrappers were spread on the floor beside them, their champagne in the heavy tumblers from beside the water carafe. Paul had checked on Daniel briefly to find him still asleep but felt the need to stay in the hospital overnight. Sarah had agreed completely.

'It's not much of a wedding night,' Paul apologised yet again.

'Let's think of it as a practice run,' Sarah suggested. 'Why don't we do it all again in a few months when all this is behind us? We'll have a big party and I'll get a real wedding dress.'

'Daniel could be my groomsman,' Paul agreed.

'And Luke could be a flower-dog.'

'And we could have a honeymoon on a desert island with nothing to do but make love.'

'Mmm.' Sarah and Paul eyed each other.

'Sarah?'

'Yes?' She pressed her lips together and tried to match his serious expression.

'Do you think our marriage certificate will be valid in a court of law if it's unconsummated?'

Sarah tilted her head thoughtfully. 'I don't think so.'

'Perhaps we should do something about that.' Paul's face was close to hers. So close she could feel the movement of his lips as he spoke.

'Absolutely,' she murmured, just before speech became impossible. 'It's our duty.'

It was nearly dawn when Sarah let herself back into her apartment and hung up her now very crumpled dress and jacket. She decided against trying to sleep. A long, hot shower and a cup of strong coffee were all she needed. She found herself smiling.

'It might have been an unusual wedding night,' she told her empty apartment, 'but it was certainly memorable.'

Holding out her left hand, Sarah glanced at the rings. Paul had produced her engagement ring again and had insisted that she put it on. 'It wasn't the world's greatest engagement, was it?' he'd said ruefully.

'An engagement is only an entrée,' Sarah had replied. 'We never needed that, did we?'

'Don't ever take it off again,' Paul had warned.

'Perhaps I should—just for a while.' Sarah had frowned. 'Daniel's not going to be too happy about this.'

Paul had shaken his head. 'This is a new beginning. For all of us. No half-measures and no deception. Our relationship is the base that we're going to build our future on and that includes Daniel's future, I hope. What sort of message would it give him if it looks like it's up for negotiation or adjustment?'

Sarah nodded to herself now. He was absolutely right. She rinsed out her coffee-cup hurriedly. It was just as well she wasn't working at present. She was going to have a very busy few days.

The first priority was a visit to her family. Her parents' disappointment at the secrecy of her marriage was not completely dispelled by her explanation of the need for haste and the situation not being appropriate for a large celebration. Her mother was, however, mollified by the idea of a repeat ceremony in the near future.

'You could have it here in the garden,' Evelyn suggested. 'In spring, when all the bulbs and blossom are out.'

'Sounds great,' Sarah agreed. 'I've got a few other things to organise first, though. You don't know of any houses to rent out of town, do you? Not quite as far as this but we'll need plenty of room for Luke. And good fences.'

'I'll ask at the clinic,' Jack told her. 'My receptionist knows everybody for miles.'

'And I'll make a few phone calls,' Evelyn promised. 'There's bound to be a farm cottage empty somewhere.'

Having set those wheels in motion, Sarah made the trip back to town and to the hospital. Paul was in his office. The backlog of work from his time spent at Daniel's bedside was beginning to present problems.

'Daniel's angry now,' he told Sarah, 'but he's not ready to talk. I've been with him all morning but I had to get some work done and he kept telling me to go away and leave me alone.'

'Did you tell him about us, getting married?'

'Of course.'

'How did he take it?'

Paul shrugged. 'Hard to tell. He's angry with everything and everybody. You, me, himself and especially his mother. Not that he would admit it.'

'It's part of the grief process,' Sarah said. 'It's the death of a dream for him.'

'I know.' Paul sighed. 'But it's not easy to know how to help in the face of rejection.'

'Don't let it get to you,' Sarah advised. 'The most important thing is to weather the storm, be there for him and let him know how much you love him.'

Paul nodded. 'I'm doing my best, Doc.'

'How is he physically?'

'He looks terrible. Hung-over from the sedative and emotional grinder. He refused to do any physiotherapy. Cheryl was going to take him swimming. We've postponed the final scan as well. I think it'll be a few days before he can be discharged.'

'Good. I need time to organise somewhere for us

to live.' Sarah moved towards the office door. 'I'll go and see him now.'

The destruction of the bond that Sarah and Daniel had built was evident the moment Sarah entered the boy's room.

'Go away,' he told her. 'I'm busy.' His eyes were glued to the screen of the small television they had installed in his room. A cartoon show was playing. Loudly.

'Can I turn the TV down and talk to you for a minute?'

'No.' Daniel's head didn't turn. Sarah sat on the end of his bed. At least he couldn't have too much of a headache, Sarah decided, if he could stand the television at this volume. She wasn't surprised when Angela put her head through the doorway.

'Turn it down, thanks, Daniel. Or use the ear-plugs. You're disturbing some sick kids.'

With a theatrical sigh Daniel climbed out of his bed and put the earplug jack into the socket. He then began to untangle the long wire. Sarah took advantage of the sudden silence.

'I'm really sorry your mother didn't come, Daniel.'

'I'm not,' Daniel snapped. 'I don't care.'

'Well, I care,' Sarah told him. 'I can understand why you're angry and I want you to know that I care about how you feel.'

'Go away,' Daniel told her again. He had straightened the wire and he climbed back onto his bed as he inserted the earplugs. 'I don't need a mother,' he said loudly, unable to hear his own voice. 'And I don't want one.'

Sarah sat for a while but there was no communication possible. Daniel hunched himself up in the bed so that his back was towards her. His eyes were fixed on the television again and there was no way he could hear her. With a sigh Sarah stood up. She'd known it wouldn't be easy but she felt as though she were facing a brick wall. Her heart sank even further on leaving Daniel's room.

A rubbish bin stood beside the door. Along with a bunch of dead flowers and some screwed-up papers, a soft toy was wedged into the bin. A scruffy dog with black spots.

The location of a suitable cottage didn't present the obstacle Sarah had feared it might. The location was perfect, just out of the city limits, the fencing ideal to keep a young dog contained and the acre of garden and orchard a paradise for both a puppy and a child. The state of the long-unoccupied house was far from ideal.

That weekend saw Sarah, her parents, Helen and Holly and several friends involved in an intensive cleaning-up operation. Paul came for an hour or two when he could spare the time from work pressures and being with his son. He always seemed to arrive just when everyone was stopping for a meal or coffee-break, which caused some friendly ribbing.

'Start as you mean to go on, that's what I say,' Paul countered. 'I am a manager after all.'

'You'll keep,' Sarah warned him, going past with an armload of rotting curtains. Then she caught the look in Paul's eyes and bit her lip. She knew how increasingly frustrating he was finding his employment. He dreamed of returning to surgery but was convinced it would have to stay a dream.

'It's been too long now,' he'd told her sadly. 'I haven't even done a locum in more than a year. I'm out of touch. My confidence has gone.'

'It would come back,' Sarah had assured him. 'It's just a matter of taking that step.'

'No.' Paul had shaken his head. 'There's a lot more to it. Thanks to Daniel's accident. I felt so helpless when that happened. It's not just the victim's life that's hanging in the balance and dependent on medical skill. I was just as dependent on an emotional level. For each victim or patient there's a whole network of people affected. I just didn't realise how deep that could go. It makes the responsibility feel overwhelming. I don't think I could ever take it on again.'

Sarah had been unable to persuade Paul and had dropped the subject for the moment. Seeing the look in his eyes now made her determined to raise it again—soon. There had to be some way to make him change his mind and pursue the career he so desperately missed. Some way to give him back the confidence that Daniel's emergency had shaken out of him. Right at this moment, however, there were more urgent tasks. Sarah shoved the pile of rotten fabric into Paul's arms.

'Here. Manage these for me. They're to go on the trailer. Dad's doing a trip to the rubbish dump later.'

A muffled voice came from the depths of a kitchen cupboard.

'What's that, Mum?'

Evelyn backed away from her task, scrubbing brush in hand. 'I said I put the old curtains from our attic in the back of my car. See if you can find a set to fit. They're old, but they're clean.'

Holly came skipping down the wide hallway. 'There's a henhouse in the orchard.'

'Great.' Sarah smiled. 'Daniel will love that.' She grinned and waved at Angela who was washing the outside of the windows. 'Come in for coffee!' she called.

'I still can't believe you got married, without asking me.'

'You've grumbled about that ever since you got here Angela. I keep telling you we'll do it again.'

'Can I be a bridesmaid?' Holly spoke around a mouthful of muffin.

'You'd have to be Daniel's partner,' Sarah pointed out. 'And not wind him up.'

Holly considered this. 'That's cool,' she pronounced. 'I suppose he's part of the family now. I'll only wind him up on Saturdays.'

'So, when is it to be?' Angela persisted. 'I want to make a note in my diary.'

'Why?' Sarah grinned. 'So you don't get double-booked?'

Angela groaned. 'I wish. Still, my love life is not the issue. Let's see. You're too late for Easter and Christmas is too far away—'

'It doesn't matter,' Sarah interrupted. 'It'll be special whenever we do it.'

'I know.' Angela snapped her fingers. 'Mother's Day. You are becoming an instant mother after all.'

Sarah caught Paul's eye and they exchanged a

wry glance. She was about as far away from being
Daniel's mother at present than she could ever be.
His anger had faded, to be replaced by a sullen
reserve. He had returned to clinging to his relationship with his father and made sure Sarah felt unwelcome whenever she came near. It was lucky she
was simply too busy to let it get her down, Sarah
thought. On top of the clean-up of the house, the
apartments had had to be packed up. The removal
trucks were due on Monday, the day before Daniel
was going to be discharged.

Sarah and Paul had discussed the pros and cons
of not taking Daniel back to his old home at great
length. They'd decided that the length of time he'd
been in hospital was going to mean adjustment in
any case, and to settle him and then shift him again
shortly afterwards would only add to his insecurity.

'It's part of the base,' Paul had reminded Sarah.
'Let's make sure it's secure.'

Angela broke into Sarah's thoughts. 'So? What
do you think? A Mother's Day wedding?'

Evelyn came to Sarah's rescue. 'That's only three
weeks away. I couldn't possibly organise anything
by then. No, it has to be spring.'

Three weeks away. Sarah knew the date would
hang over her much as the time of Catherine's
planned visit had done—an event to mark how far
away they were from being a real family.

An event to mark how she wasn't—and could
never be—Daniel's mother.

CHAPTER TEN

'IF I SAY you can't then you can't. So there!'

'Maybe I don't want to.'

'You do too. And you can't.'

'Who said you're the boss?'

'I'm older than you. And you're just a nerd.'

'Well. You're a *girl*!'

The verdict was given with the tone of an ultimate insult and Sarah shook her head. The quarrel between the children was drifting in through the window of the kitchen where she and Evelyn were finishing the preparations for a family lunch. She sighed lightly and stopped rinsing the lettuce as the conversation faded. Then the voices rose again as Holly and Daniel came inside the house.

'We'll ask, then.'

'You won't be allowed. You just wait and see.'

The children entered the kitchen. Evelyn looked up from where she sat at the table, buttering bread rolls.

'I wouldn't put your nose that far up in the air if I were you, Holly. You'll leak when it rains.' Evelyn watched Daniel who stood with his eyes down. Luke sat on the floor beside him, stretching his shoelace to breaking point. 'What's the problem, Daniel?'

The boy glanced up. 'Holly says I'm not allowed

169

to call you Gran. She says that you're her grand-mother and not mine.'

'Oh.' Evelyn Kendall put down her knife. 'As far as I'm concerned, Daniel, you're as much a part of my family now as Holly is. Would you like to call me Gran?'

Daniel hesitated and then nodded slightly. Holly looked put out but shrugged and flashed a cheeky grin at Sarah.

'It's Saturday,' she pronounced. Evelyn gave her a stern look but turned back to Daniel. 'Of course, there are important things about having a gran that you should know,' she told Daniel seriously.

Daniel's suspicious scowl was automatic. 'What's that?'

'They need lots of cuddles.'

Sarah held her breath as Evelyn opened her arms. Her mouth dropped open a little as she saw Daniel willingly go into her mother's embrace, and she was aware of a wave of jealousy. How could it be so easy for her mother to gain acceptance when Daniel refused to let Sarah herself even try to get close? She shook the lettuce leaves so vigorously that the stalks snapped off as she stared out the window, watching the children running back out-side, the fat puppy waddling in their wake. Daniel looked happier than she had seen him since—well, since the day she'd brought him out to meet her parents for the first time.

'How come it's so easy for you?' she asked Evelyn wistfully. 'I'm trying so hard and he won't even talk to me, let alone let me give him a cuddle.'

'Perhaps you're trying too hard,' Evelyn suggested. 'Relax a little. Children need to know their limits and they need a lot of love, that's all. Especially Daniel. He's going to need a lot of love for a long time.'

'I've got a lot to give him. He just won't accept it.' Sarah put the salad bowl on the table.

'He will,' Evelyn said complacently. 'He's desperate for it. I'm just safer, that's all. I'm not competing with him for his father's attention and he doesn't have to think about me as a mother figure.'

'Huh!' Sarah snorted. 'He thinks of me as simply a live-in maid. I asked him to pick up his clothes in the bathroom the other night and do you know what he said? "You do it—that's *your* job." '

'He's just testing the limits,' her mother told her. 'You need to be kind but firm. Children have to have limits so they can feel secure within them. If you're consistent and he can push so far and can't win or drive you away then he'll feel it's safe to accept you. Then the love can really begin.'

'It's not so much his rudeness to me that bothers me,' Sarah said. 'It's the way I get between him and Paul. He told Paul that he'd rather have a housekeeper because at least she would live somewhere else. Paul got angry and told him off and so the tension just keeps increasing.'

'It's only been three weeks,' Evelyn smiled.

'It feels like three years,' Sarah groaned. 'It's a bit easier since he's gone back to school, though. At least we have one thing in common now.'

'What's that?'

'The sense of relief when Paul gets home,' Sarah said sadly.

The shrieks of children's laughter from the orchard made them both smile. 'It's wonderful to see him looking so well,' Evelyn said.

Sarah nodded. 'The recovery power of kids never ceases to amaze me. He hasn't even had a headache since he came out of hospital, and with his hair growing back you'd never know it had happened.'

'That gives us two things to celebrate, then. Cheer up, love, and get the bubbly out of the fridge. I'll see if the others have the barbecue under control.'

Sarah took the cold bottle of champagne and began to undo the foil wrapping. The children were the only ones not to know the reason for this celebration lunch. Court proceedings had dragged on over the last three weeks but yesterday final ruling had been given. Catherine had no grounds on which to gain custody. Paul and Sarah had sole and permanent responsibility for Daniel's upbringing. Access visits had been offered but only within New Zealand. Much to everyone's relief, the offer had been declined.

'If she can't have it all, she won't want any of it,' Paul had commented. 'Thank God for that.'

The barbecue smelled wonderful and Sarah watched Daniel as he pointed out to Paul which sausages he wanted.

'I'll have that one. And that one with the burnt bits. You're the best cook, Dad.'

'I specialise in burnt bits,' Paul agreed. He grinned at Sarah and she responded, trying to quell the pang it gave her. Daniel only picked at any meals she created. She tried to conjure up some optimism as she continued to watch father and son, happily sorting the meats, but failed miserably. The day she had been dreading was almost upon them. Tomorrow was Mother's Day and she had made no progress at all with Daniel. If anything, their relationship had deteriorated.

The peaceful rural surroundings added to the air of anticipation as the meal preparations were completed. Sarah was beginning to pour the champagne when the peace was jarred by the distant roar of a vehicle.

Paul groaned. 'The louts are out.'

Jack shook his head with disbelief. 'If people had any sense at all they'd have some respect for gravel roads. Instead, we get idiots who think they're on some sort of car rally.'

They all stopped to listen as the crescendo of noise peaked and then began to fade.

'I hate to think what speed he was doing,' Paul began, when suddenly he stopped. The noise of the vehicle had cut out as though a switch had been flicked. A split second later there was an horrendous thump and a scraping noise.

'It's rolled,' Paul stated calmly. 'He was going too fast to take the bend.' He was already moving towards his car. Sarah was surprised to see him pull a solid case out of the boot of his car. 'I didn't know you kept an emergency kit,' she exclaimed.

Paul flashed her a wry smile as he started to run. 'I like to pretend I'm still a doctor,' he called back over his shoulder.

'Just as well,' Jack muttered. 'For once I haven't got mine with me.'

Sarah set off at a run to catch up with Paul. Jack went to his car, having told the others to stay put. By the time he'd negotiated the long driveway Sarah and Paul were already at the scene, having cut across the field. The car was back on its wheels, the roof heavily dented. The single occupant, a young male, was slumped over the top of the steering-wheel.

'No safety belt,' muttered Paul. He tried the driver's door but it was jammed. Jack arrived at that point and took a crowbar from his boot. The door came open with a metallic screech a few seconds later. Paul's hand went to the carotid artery on the victim's neck.

'He's alive,' he told Sarah. 'Call an ambulance.'

Sarah picked up the cellphone and spoke into it as she watched Paul. He held his hand in front of the man's nose and then leaned his own head in closer.

'Mild stridor,' he told Jack. He began gently feeling the victim's head and neck. 'No obvious fractures but we'll have to watch his neck. The bleeding seems to be superficial—from that scalp laceration.' Paul leaned closer again but the laboured breathing sounds could now be heard even by Sarah who was standing some distance away. Paul straightened briefly. 'We're going to have to get him out or he'll asphyxiate. Sarah, you and Jack will have to try and stabilise his head and neck while I lift out the lower half.'

Jack positioned himself beside Paul, and Sarah climbed into the passenger seat. Slowly and awkwardly they managed to move their patient, with

Sarah crawling over the seats as she tried to splint the neck with her hands.

'On the road,' Paul ordered breathlessly. 'We need a flat surface.' He stripped off his jersey, rolling it up and placing it under the hollow of the victim's neck. 'Find some more padding,' he directed Sarah. 'Try and get something right around his head.' Paul opened his emergency kit and quickly put on surgical gloves. Taking an oral airway, he inserted it into the patient's mouth but the laboured breathing continued unchanged.

'Look at that.' Paul touched the obvious bruising on the man's throat. He felt around the area carefully. 'I think he's fractured the hyoid bone. There's a lot of contusion. We're going to have to do a tracheostomy.'

Jack looked doubtful. 'Here? I don't think my skills are up to that.'

'Mine are.' Paul began to pull items from his kit as he spoke. 'You support his head. Don't extend the neck any further than it is now. Put one hand around the back of his head and one under his chin. Sarah, you hold the sides.'

Holding an alcohol swab in one hand, Paul carefully felt down the victim's neck. His fingers found the V-shaped depression at the top of the adam's apple, ran down and located the ring of cartilage beneath. He swabbed the area and reached for a scalpel and a large-gauge IV cannula. Sarah watched in admiration as Paul confidently made a stab incision just above the ring of cartilage and then deftly inserted the cannula. He removed the central part to leave a hollow tube.

'Grab the scissors, Sarah—get his shirt off.' Paul was checking the air flow of the tube. He reached for his stethoscope.

'There's several broken ribs on the right side,' Sarah informed him.

Paul was listening to the chest over the top of the collar-bones. 'He's got a broken right collar-bone and a pneumothorax.'

Jack groaned. He had his hand on the side of the victim's neck. 'Pulse rate's going up,' he commented.

Paul made a rapid survey. 'Doesn't look like any major limb fractures. How's his abdomen?'

'No obvious distension,' Sarah reported.

'Look at this.' Paul's attention went back to the man's chest. 'Surgical emphysema!'

Sarah touched the skin. Air under pressure had been forced into the subcutaneous tissue. It felt like the bubble paper used to wrap parcels. Even as she felt it she was aware of the increased efforts at respiration under her hand. Paul was checking the tracheostomy tube. He shook his head.

'He's losing it. It must be a tension pneumothorax.' He began to listen to the chest again, rapidly moving position from top to bottom and back again. 'Grab me another angiocath, Sarah. We can't do this from the side—I don't want to move him. We'll go for a high intercostal space.' Paul seemed to be talking to himself and Sarah was astonished at the speed and confidence with which he moved. Another stab incision was made between the patient's ribs and the internal part of the cannula again removed after insertion to provide a hollow tube. A rush of air signalled the release of the trapped air which had collapsed one lung and threatened the function of the other.

'I'll put a three-way tap on this and a syringe,' Paul stated. 'We can release any further air that way.'

'Heart rate's dropping,' Jack said with relief. 'And the pulse volume's on the way up.'

Paul straightened. He flashed a grin at Sarah. They could hear the wail of the ambulance in the distance now.

'We'll get an IV line in and run in a litre of haemaccel.'

Sarah handed him another swab and IV cannula. 'You're wasted in management,' she told him. 'You belong back in Theatre.' She watched the excited light in those dark blue eyes kindle.

'You know something? I think you're absolutely right.'

The peaceful family atmosphere disintegrated following the accident. Paul went in the ambulance, determined to manage his patient on the trip back to town. Evelyn took Jack home to clean up. The blood from the accident victim's scalp wound had managed to spread itself over every item of clothing he had been wearing. Helen and Holly stayed for a while but, in the absence of Paul, Daniel's mood suffered an abrupt decline. He and Holly ended up in another argument. Of all things, it was about Mother's Day.

'I'm going to take my mum breakfast in bed,'

Holly announced when Helen was safely out of ear-shot, washing dishes. 'I've made a card, too.'

Sarah looked up from her task of tidying the bar-becue. 'Good for you,' she told her niece. 'She'll love that.'

Sarah was moving back into the house when she heard Holly ask Daniel what he was going to do for Mother's Day.

'Why should I do anything?' The reply was sul-len. 'I haven't got a mother.'

They were trading insults as Sarah retreated to the kitchen, but the silence was ominous when she returned for the last of the plates. Holly, clearly fed up with Daniel's attitude, nagged her mother until Helen gave in and took her home. Sarah understood how Holly felt.

She watched Daniel over what now seemed a very long afternoon as he played in a rather half-hearted fashion with Luke and wandered aimlessly around the property. He refused the meal Sarah pre-pared for him in the evening and it was difficult not to show a flash of real irritation. Perhaps her mother was right. She was going to have to stake out some limits. She had been too accepting of his rude be-haviour so far. Daniel responded by turning on the television and ignoring her.

They both waited for the return of Paul. He rang to tell her he was very keen to stay and observe the imminent surgery on his patient, having success-fully managed the difficult case himself on the way in. It was obvious he had gained enormous satis-faction from the successful resuscitation and any lack of confidence in his abilities had been completely erased. Sarah did her best to encourage the excitement he was allowing himself at the prospect of returning to surgery.

'It could be perfect timing,' he told Sarah during the phone call. 'There's a general surgical position coming up in a few months' time, I'm told. That would give me enough time to do some retraining.'

'You don't need it,' Sarah told him. 'And I think you should go for it. It's what you should have been doing all along.'

'But what about the longer hours? The on-call?' Paul reminded her. His tone held a plea that Sarah responded to firmly.

'We'll manage. I've told Martin Lynch I'll only work in his private practice during school hours and I need to have school holidays free as well. He's quite happy with that. Even if we have other children we can still work around that.'

'Not if. When,' Paul told her happily. 'Nothing can stop us now.'

Sarah hung up, feeling delighted that Paul was so excited about the future and the idea of returning to the work he loved. The atmosphere of the house, after terminating their contact, suddenly increased her own frustration, however. The prospect of having their own children should have been a very exciting one, but the way things were at present it wasn't possible to even contemplate the idea seriously.

She told Daniel that Paul was on his way home.

'Good,' he replied, his relief patent. He didn't look away from the television.

Sarah fed Luke and then put a tray of steak and

sausages left over from the barbecue into the oven
to reheat. Paul would be starving. She sighed loudly
as the laughter from the television show jarred her
mood. The volume had been annoying Sarah for
some time and she had been ignored twice in her
request to have it turned down. So much for my
ability to set limits, she thought miserably. When
the advertisement for the chocolates that promised
to be the perfect Mothers' Day gift came on, however, Sarah finally snapped. She marched into the
room, grabbed the remote control and pushed the
mute button. Daniel was enraged.

'Turn it back on! I was watching that!'

'No, I won't turn it back on, Daniel. I've had
enough. I asked you to turn it down twice and you
ignored me.'

'I don't have to do what you tell me.' Daniel's
eyes flashed. He looked exactly like his father had
the time Sarah accused him of having an affair with
her. Daniel scrambled to his knees, his fists
clenched, and Sarah stared down at the angry little
face. 'You can't tell me what to do,' he shouted up
at her. 'You're *not* my mother. I don't need a
mother.'

Sarah's anger fled. As she held the eye contact
with Daniel she could suddenly see past the surface
aggression. She could see the vulnerability and the
pain. She could see a small child desperately trying
to make sense of the emotional war in which he
was engaged. Sarah dropped to a crouch in front of
him, still holding the first direct eye contact they'd
had in a very long time.

'No, I'm not your mother, Daniel,' she said quietly. 'I didn't give birth to you. But there's more to being a mother than giving birth.' Sarah took a deep breath as Daniel looked away, but she wasn't going to stop now.

'It's about loving a child, caring very much about what happens to him. Being happy because he's happy. Being sad because he's sad. Trying to help him become the best person he can be and worrying about whether the choices made are the right ones. Especially just being there—no matter what. Maybe that's being a mum, rather than a mother.'

Daniel was sitting very still but his head was turned away. Sarah couldn't be sure he was even listening but she felt compelled to continue.

'You don't need a mother—but I think you would like to have a mum. You haven't had anybody you could trust enough to be that before. You have now. I'm not going anywhere, Daniel. I married your dad because I love him very, very much. I made a promise to stay with him and love him for the rest of my life. That promise included you. It doesn't matter if you give me a hard time and make life difficult for me. Well, it does matter because it makes all of us unhappy and stops us being a family, but it's not going to make me go away. Ever. We could be a family—that's up to you.'

Sarah sighed and sat down on the floor. She waited out the silence, hoping Daniel would say something. But the silence continued until Sarah broke it.

'You know, when a mother gives birth to a baby she feels an incredible joy—and anxiety. The first thing she wants to know is whether the baby's OK.

If it is she can feel all the hope for the future of that baby, the love she can give and receive and the excitement of knowing she can watch that baby grow up and become a special person.

'When you were so sick in hospital I sat and watched you and worried about whether you would be OK. When you woke up I felt so happy—as happy as the day I knew your dad loved me as much as I loved him. And I felt that hope for your future. And I knew I loved you.

'That love is there for you, Daniel. And you can choose whether you let it grow. It's like....' Sarah searched for an analogy. 'It's like training Luke. You have to start with the little things and then build on them. If you do it with love and under-standing and can be consistent then one day you find you have an amazing bond. An obedience champion, maybe. Or a family.' Sarah bit her lip. She had run dry finally. She felt exhausted but re-lieved. She'd said all the things she'd been wanting to say for weeks. Had he listened? Or was it too much for an eight-year-old to take on board?

When it became apparent that Sarah had finally stopped talking Daniel moved. But not towards Sarah. Very slowly, he got to his feet and, without turning, he left the room. Sarah waited until she heard his bedroom door close quietly before she let the tears come.

'It'll come,' Paul told her later that night as she lay nestled in his arms in their bed. 'I'm sure it will.'

'I feel like I've given all I can,' Sarah said mournfully. 'But it still isn't enough.'

'It's more than enough for me,' Paul murmured. 'And I love you more than I ever thought it was possible to love anyone. Will that do for the moment? For me to love you enough for both of us?'

Sarah nestled closer but said nothing. What could she say? Paul's love was perfect, more than she had dreamed of sharing. But, no, it wasn't quite enough.

Mother's Day dawned bright and clear. Sarah awoke before Paul and lay listening to the chorus of birdsong outside their window. She gently extricated her limbs from the tangle they'd been in with Paul's. He stirred and opened his eyes slowly. Then he smiled.

'You've no idea how wonderful it is—you being the first thing I see each day.'

'Oh, yes, I do.' Sarah moved closer to give him a lingering kiss. Then she propped herself up on one elbow. The scuffling noise she heard in the hall probably meant Luke needed to be let out—if it wasn't already too late.

The bedroom door was slightly ajar. Sarah watched as it slowly opened further. It *was* Luke, but he had company. Daniel came into their room, carefully balancing a large wooden tray. Looking more serious than Sarah had ever seen him, he put the tray on her bedside table.

The glass of orange juice had spilled a little. The toast was more than a little burnt. But Sarah didn't even see the culinary offerings. The only thing she was aware of on the tray was the card—a folded sheet of cardboard with a magazine picture of a dog carefully glued to the front.

Sarah reached out her hand and slowly opened

the card. The message pencilled inside was simple. It read, "Happy Mum's Day."

Sarah caught her bottom lip between her teeth as she blinked hard to prevent the prickle of joyful tears developing any further. She was aware of Paul's face very close to her own as he read the card over her shoulder.

With an effort, Sarah raised her eyes from the message on the card to find Daniel's dark blue eyes gazing at her solemnly. His expression was wary, his anticipation of her reaction palpable. Sarah held the eye contact but didn't smile.

'This is the best card I've ever, ever, had,' she told him seriously.

Daniel's expression flickered but he remained motionless—still waiting.

'Of course,' Sarah continued carefully, 'there are important things about having a mum that you should know.'

This time there was a hint of a smile in the small face. 'Are they the same as about having a gran?'

Sarah nodded as her lips began to curve into a smile.

'Well, I do know, then,' Daniel stated confidently.

'I don't.' Paul raised an eyebrow at his son. 'What are they?'

Daniel sighed with mild exasperation. 'They need lots of hugs,' he explained patiently.

'Absolutely right.' Sarah sat up and held her arms open.

She gently folded the small boy into her arms. It was as though the gift she was receiving was too

precious to risk any damage. The hug was brief.
Sarah felt suddenly nervous, not wanting to push
things too fast or too far. An unfamiliar shyness
swept over her and she could see the reaction reflected in Daniel's face. It was Paul who saved the
moment from becoming awkward. He sat up and
patted the space in the bed beside him command-
ingly.

'Come on. There's plenty of room and it's my
turn for a cuddle.'

Daniel happily scrambled over Sarah's legs and
climbed into the bed between them. Luke made an
unsuccessful attempt to follow him. Paul wrapped
his arm around his son's shoulders and then grinned
at Sarah.

'Well?'

Sarah found four very dark blue eyes regarding
her seriously.'

'Well, what?'

'Aren't you going to eat your breakfast?'

As Sarah carefully balanced the tray on her knees
Luke made a successful attempt to join them, having launched himself at the bed from a greater distance. Daniel caught the enthusiastic puppy before
he could bounce onto Sarah's tray. He looked worried.

'Is he allowed on the bed?'

'Of course,' Sarah replied. 'He's part of the family, isn't he?'

Daniel nodded, burying a happy grin in the
puppy's neck.

Paul chuckled. 'He might even get a piece of

toast. I can see Daniel's inherited my cooking speciality.'

Daniel's face appeared again, looking anxious. 'What's wrong with the toast?'

'Nothing,' Sarah said firmly. 'And I'm the only one who gets to eat it.' She shut her eyes briefly as she held a piece of toast by its blackened crust and then she sighed happily.

'This is going to be the best breakfast I've ever, ever, had.'

MILLS & BOON®

Makes any time special

Enjoy a romantic novel from Mills & Boon®

Presents™ *Enchanted*™ *Temptation*.

Historical Romance™ *Medical Romance*™

MILLS & BOON®

Medical Romance™

COMING NEXT MONTH

AN UNEXPECTED BONUS by Caroline Anderson
Bundles of Joy

Dr Ed Latimer had said he couldn't have children, but Jo was quite definitely pregnant! It was a wonderfully unexpected bonus, but Ed's reaction wasn't quite what Jo expected.

THE LOCUM AT LARCHWOOD by Janet Ferguson

Dr Kate Burnett and the locum, Guy, were beginning more than a working relationship—until her ex-boyfriend came back…

UNDO THE PAST by Gill Sanderson

Senior Registrar John Hawke could see Lauren was holding people at bay, but if he could persuade her to make him part of her life, maybe he could solve the problem.

AN UNGUARDED MOMENT by Helen Shelton

Dr Ginny Reid was shocked when her practice partner and best friend, Mark, wanted to leave. He'd been patient long enough, waiting for Ginny to understand her feelings…

Available from 2nd April 1999

FREE
2 BOOKS
AND A SURPRISE GIFT!

We would like to take this opportunity to thank you for reading this Mills & Boon® book by offering you the chance to take TWO more specially selected titles from the Medical Romance™ series absolutely FREE! We're also making this offer to introduce you to the benefits of the Reader Service™—

- ★ FREE home delivery
- ★ FREE monthly Newsletter
- ★ FREE gifts and competitions
- ★ Exclusive Reader Service discounts
- ★ Books available before they're in the shops

Accepting these FREE books and gift places you under no obligation to buy; you may cancel at any time, even after receiving your free shipment. Simply complete your details below and return the entire page to the address below. **You don't even need a stamp!**

YES! Please send me 2 free Medical Romance books and a surprise gift. I understand that unless you hear from me, I will receive 4 superb new titles every month for just £2.40 each, postage and packing free. I am under no obligation to purchase any books and may cancel my subscription at any time. The free books and gift will be mine to keep in any case.

M9EC

Ms/Mrs/Miss/Mr ....Initials ....
BLOCK CAPITALS PLEASE

Surname...

Address..

....

....Postcode ....

Send this whole page to:
THE READER SERVICE, FREEPOST CN81, CROYDON, CR9 3WZ
(Eire readers please send coupon to: P.O. Box 4546, DUBLIN 24.)

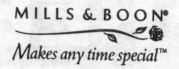

MILLS & BOON®

Makes any time special™

The Regency Collection

Mills & Boon® is delighted to bring back, for a limited period, 12 of our favourite Regency Romances for you to enjoy.

These special books will be available for you to collect each month from May, and with two full-length Historical Romance™ novels in each volume they are great value at only £4.99.

Volume One available from 7th May